V&Q
BOOKS

D0995939

Ivana Sajko, born in Zagreb in 1975, is a writer, theatre director and performer, working in the overlapping fields of literature, performance art and music. She is an author of four highly-praised novels and dozens of political theatre pieces, among which *Woman-bomb* gained international success. Her many awards include the Chevalier de l'ordre des Arts et Lettres and the HKW Internationaler Literaturpreis. She lives in Berlin.

Mima Simić is a Croatian writer, an award-winning film critic, translator and political activist. Her short stories have been included in numerous anthologies, and have been adapted for radio, TV and animated film. Her translations include works of fiction, non-fiction, literary theory, screenplays and films. She lives and works in Berlin.

LOVE NOVEL

Ivana Sajko

Translated from Croatian by Mima Simić

V&Q BOOKS

Creative Europe

Co-funded by the Creative Europe
programme of the European Union

V&Q Books, Berlin 2022
An imprint of Verlag Voland & Quist GmbH
First published in the Croatian language as *Ljubavni roman*
by Ivana Sajko
© Meandarmedia, Zagreb 2015

Translation © Mima Simić
Editing: Katy Derbyshire
Copy editing: Angela Hirons
Cover photo: Unsplash
Cover design: Pingundpong*Gestaltungsbüro
Typesetting: Fred Uhde
Printing and binding: PBtisk, Příbram, Czech Republic

ISBN: 978-3-86391-330-4

www.vq-books.eu

This book was written in Graz, Pula and sometimes Zagreb, with the generous support of Kulturvermittlung Steiermark, and thanks to a Jean-Jacques Rousseau fellowship. I wish to thank Luise and the ghost of Cerrini, who watched over our temporary home, as well as Tomi and Ivana, who graciously let us use theirs. With the greatest tenderness, I dedicate this book to Yves, and to the loved ones around him.

1

WORDS, WORDS, WORDS, he screamed at the top of his lungs; the first thing that came to his mind when he finally managed to cut through her breathless sentences – he didn't even try to understand what she was actually saying; her hot breath against his ear had woken him up with the irritating persistence of an alarm clock, and he wanted to crush it with his fist, so he roared words, words, words, like a man who couldn't bear the ringing any more, like a man who, to tell the truth, could no longer bear her nearness either, her mouth, the hot steam it oozed; he roared with the force of a scorched man, as if she'd burned him, and for a moment she thought the roar would bring the walls down, so she cowered, covered her head with her hands, dug her fingers in her hair and squeezed her eyes shut 'til it hurt, reacting like a typical female, typical by his standards, meaning excessive, hysterical and self-destructive, since she deliberately pulled her hair out, deliberately curled up in the pose of a crushed alarm clock and forced tears to her eyes as if to take revenge on him with this classic scene of domestic violence. She staged it in a second, lifting her weeping face towards him, towards the ceiling, towards the sky, and protecting herself with her fists full of tufts of pulled-out hair.

It didn't impress him.

It didn't suit her either.

She's capable of coming up with something far more disgusting.

Just opening her mouth would do it. But he won't let her.

He stirs like a volcano, lava boiling in his cheeks; he raises his hand in a frenzy, he raises his hand, he raises his hand and… he stops himself, because the blow would hurt her more if it were shaped into a word, a thunderous and meaningless word that thrashes in all directions and won't be drowned out, and so again he hollers words, words, words, and indeed words are now thundering around the room, throughout the whole flat, or to be more precise, the cramped two-room apartment they're renting at too high a price, so that most of their eruptions could be explained away by the fact they're once again late with the rent. Demoralising, but true.

She'd imagined them in more relaxed circumstances, and with much more floor space.

He admitted that she'd drawn the shittiest straw.

But better not to revisit that topic.

Not now. Because the words are in the room.

Words comparable to quicksand. Crumbling between their teeth, getting crushed into slimy sand, slipping from their lips like muddy bubbles with no meaningful content. Dripping down their chins. They should both look in the mirror and commit the image to memory. To make them sick of it. But they won't. They'd rather keep the mud gurgling until they run out of oxygen, until their last bubbles dribble down to the floorboards and they finally mop them up; they can't live in a pigsty, after all. Only then will they glance at themselves in the mirror, wipe the secretions off their chins and the smudged mascara from their eyes, comb their hair, fix their clothes, inhale, exhale, and expire. You might indeed say: they'll expire in yet another death, a tragic case of drowning in the bullshit they regularly step in, like true and passionate suicides. But she won't be the one to reach for the mop first, no she won't; she'll let the mud form a crust on the floor for him to see what his words, words, words really look like, up close.

But surely he must be aware of how stupid it is to be repeating words, words, words, without actually saying anything; and just demonstrating that every word is meaningless, and too loud, besides? Isn't he, in fact, trying to convey that they no longer have anything to say to each other and that there was no justifiable reason to wake him from a dream, a well-deserved dream, mind you, with which he'd been trying to cure his unyielding exhaustion, his cursed frantic life with its impending rents that make him age ten years in a month; and just look at him; he's already a hundred, two hundred, three hundred, it's been too much for way too long now, and if she really wants to know, he too had imagined more relaxed circumstances, quiet afternoons of digesting his dinner on the couch, dozing off with his feet resting on the coffee table and waking up during the evening news; he'd imagined things would take care of themselves, or at least that he wouldn't feel guilty if they didn't, and he really didn't expect random acquaintances to be asking concerned questions about his health because he seems so exhausted, withered and fucked up, because he looks like he has a tumour and not just a woman, this woman who always fights back twice as hard, as if to say: man, you sure drew a shitty straw, too. The shittiest. And then she adds that no one would ever love him as much as she loves him. He'd better remember that.

Nobody.

Ever.

As much as me.

He can't stand it any more. He can't handle such a high concentration of contradictory sentences, without going crazy or getting plastered. He needs to get some sleep. He needs to crawl into the fold of the couch, urgently; disconnect, reset himself, and forget she's nearly killed him with her love again. Indeed, he does this regularly; he falls asleep like a sick man, he curls up around an imaginary tumour and blankets himself with a grimace of ill humour. And she sees the silent pain pacing across his face, she saw it moments ago and felt sorry for him, he looked like he needed an ambulance so she decided to walk over to him, stroke his hair and whisper to him that, just below their window, a pair of sparrows were building a nest; she wanted to share this beautiful image of love, birds' devotedness, nature's balance, or something like that, and tell him it's a sure sign that spring is coming and the heating bill might be lower from next month. She wanted to tell him one thing, but he heard something different, and he raised his hand and roared words, words, words, and she lifted her face to the sky with the same expression he'd had until a moment ago; she thought of the sparrows, frightened, flying out of a treetop, and then she stood up, shook the tufts of hair from her hands, ran to the other room and slammed the door as hard as she could.

She didn't mean to do this, but now it's too late. The child is already standing up in the cot, afraid. The baby thought it was all a dream, of an earthquake or a volcanic eruption, but then the room shook for real. The child looked at her as if seeing her for the first time, and she pulled the tiny body into her arms, whispering it was safe, that Mummy had come, Mummy's here, and yet this still didn't sound like particularly good news. But the child has no choice and huddles close to her, or rather, she huddles up to the child, rocking them both and repeating that everything is all right, it's just a draught shaking the furniture and slamming the doors. Look out the window and you'll see the wind bending the branches.

All this will pass, she tells the child.

Someday we'll laugh at all this.

We'll only remember the little things; the view from the window, the spring snow and other small wonders. The way an empty nest swayed in the bent cypress tree on the other side of the windowpane, and how the sparrows fluttered across the car park. They'll remember the white image of that car park, and the slope with frosted fruit trees, and the kindergarten run by the nuns from the nearby convent. The nuns would come out, wrapped in scarves and long coats, with shovels to clear the snow from the garden paths, and then, like a funeral procession, one behind the other, they'd walk back towards the chapel.

Listen to them sing.

She explains to the child that the nuns also have a child, called Jesus. Every day they pray for his health, they decorate him with dog daisies, they wipe the dust off his pedestal, and coat him with marble polish, because Baby Jesus cares for those who serve him; he protects the poor, the sick and the downtrodden, and he teaches them to endure hardships with a smile and to keep believing that someday their troubles will disappear. Someday the kingdom will be ours.

Maybe when you're grown up?

The child listens patiently as she talks about Jesus in the same way she talks about gravity, electricity, and dolphins. And it doesn't matter that she knows nothing about either physics or electrics, that she's never seen a dolphin, or that she doesn't believe in Jesus – what matters is that it sounds like a fairy tale.

And then the bells ring out.

It's time for Mass.

At the third stroke, he opens the door quietly. He doesn't come in. He's afraid he'll step into some shit on the floor again. He watches them from behind and imagines walking over to them, stroking the child's hair, putting a conciliatory hand on her shoulder, and she'll tilt her head and run her cheek across his arm, like cats do, or women who don't hold grudges; and then they'll all stand together in front of the frosty window, thinking peaceful thoughts of snow and milk. At some point she'll turn to him and tell him the little sparrows have returned to the nest after all. He'll nod appreciatively, even though he has no idea what she's talking about, but it doesn't matter – what matters is that it will sound like a fairy tale.

2

PEOPLE SHOULD LIVE IN PEACE AND HARMONY; those were their neighbour's first words. He didn't even say hello, he just launched into his lecture as if afraid the door might be slammed in his face before he'd finished saying what he rang the bell to say. And he'd been ringing it for five minutes at least – which seemed like an hour to him. They'd even managed to start a fight, assuming the third-floor neighbour was there to scold them for not having paid their share for the staircase lighting, or for shirking their turn to clear the snow at the entrance. He hadn't been too keen on freezing his arse off in the parking lot, and she'd forgotten to put the money in the neighbour's letterbox. So she forgot, so what? They stood silently in the hallway, staring each other down.

The bell went quiet for a moment.

Maybe he's gone?

Maybe he's…

Then it buzzed again, and she just shrugged and disappeared into the kitchen, as if it was his job to make amends for her mistakes. He took another look through the peephole and mussed up his hair. He wanted to look like he'd just woken up.

So, he finally opens the door. The neighbour's standing there in his slippers, skipping polite hellos and going straight for the line about peace and harmony. He mentions neither the snow at the entrance nor the unpaid bill but goes on to say how in these difficult times people should foster good intentions and take more responsibility for their actions. So that things don't get even worse. He nods in agreement with everything the neighbour says, hoping to shut the door as soon as possible. But the neighbour is faster; he steps into the hallway with his slippered foot and gets into his face, warning him he's not done yet. He doesn't raise his voice; he just starts talking faster.

We should all be more responsible and conscientious, he says; not you personally, of course, not you, I mean in general, because you are, no doubt, already conscientious. The neighbour has noticed his habit of leaving deposit bottles near the waste containers. People have started loitering around the rubbish containers, understandably, since they find something by the bins every day. And now they come regularly to collect the stuff left there, and when they don't find anything, they go searching inside the containers, digging and diving… you've got them used to it, the neighbour tells him. And undoubtedly, it's very admirable for him to have in mind how much the deposit money might mean to some people, but the rubbish is right next to the kindergarten fence, and the children see what's going on, all that human despair and deprivation.

Shouldn't we be protecting them from it?

The neighbour repeats the question, almost rhetorically, so he naturally doesn't answer it. He shields himself with sleepiness while thinking his own thoughts, completely uninterested in other people's children and utterly unaffected by the sight of human despair and deprivation. These are everyday scenes. He's seen worse on television. His only worry right now is this neighbour's fucking slipper stuck in the door. He wants to tell him to back off, to get off his fucking case; he wants to remind him it's 8 a.m. and to suggest he come back in an hour, or never, but he will refrain – he's way too polite, even though she keeps claiming the opposite. He's leaning on the door handle, rubbing his eyes.

This will pass.

Last night your wife left a bag with a coat in it out there, the neighbour continues, that red coat she wore when she was pregnant, and this morning, just a little while ago to be precise, two guys were at each other's throats over it, you'd think they'd kill each other, while the children could see it all through the fence; the men cursed and yelled until one of them punched the other on the chin, kicked him in the gut and shoved him against the containers, and then dumped the stuff he was carrying in his bags on top of him. There's now rubbish scattered all across the car park, and I wonder if it's really worth it, exposing children to violence and misery for a few plastic bottles and an old maternity coat... you tell me.

Well?

Is it?

The neighbour should be thankful he's not responding to any of this; he's been trained to endure such crap in silence. He can handle vast amounts of stupid and tone-deaf sentences without a single twitch of a nerve, without actually hearing them. He can listen to one thing and think of another; for instance, he can imagine the neighbour having a cup of tea with bread and margarine, observing the fight outside the building, then resolutely wiping his mouth and heading off two floors down without even putting his shoes on, with the ferocity of a man who feels it's his duty to do something. And the neighbour knows exactly which doorbell he's going to be pummelling, it's not his first time, no it isn't, he'd come making demands at this doorstep before, and so he remembered he had to be persistent because, sooner or

15

later, a bleary-eyed face would open the door, the same face that doesn't obey the house rules, doesn't clear the snow, doesn't pay electricity bills or recycle bottles, and instead – as he plainly described it a moment ago – lays out his rubbish to fuel violence and misery, enough to spoil your breakfast. The neighbour keeps tabs on all the tenants, and he has undoubtedly already added up all this tenant's thrown-away wine bottles, divided them into glasses and figured out he's drinking too much. The neighbour could also tell from the label that he'd bought the wine on sale at a nearby discount store, a whole case for the price of a regular bottle, meaning it was either totally disgusting or toxic, and no one would drink it if they had a choice. And he didn't. But he had no intention of justifying himself as to why. The neighbour has already made up his mind about his bad habits and his own noble intentions, and it's way too late to try to make a good impression. He doesn't even need to wash his face. Maybe he could rub his eyes a little more. Out of sheer defiance.

The neighbour already thinks sleepiness is an expression of laziness, rather than exhaustion.

The neighbour also thinks exhaustion is a sign of weakness, rather than a side-effect of honest work.

The neighbour believes an honest day's work nets an honest day's pay.

But that's not how it goes.

Nonetheless, the neighbour knows him better than he knows himself.

And surely remembers what he himself would rather forget.

He thinks of his wife with the smooth ball under her red coat, throwing away the portable TV she thought was responsible for their communication breakdown. At least that's how she phrased it. After pointing out that him watching the evening news on three different channels in a row had nothing to do with being better informed and everything to do with wanting to escape from what was going on, mostly from her and the ball under her coat, she'd pulled the cord out of the socket, lifted the set up against her stomach and carried it out. He was afraid she'd go into labour. He sat on the couch all that night, staring into the silent gap in the place of the TV set, trying not to smoke a whole pack. She sat right there with him. She was waiting for them to start having fun. In vain. She stroked her stomach and faked a cough, growing increasingly unhappy. He was seeing static. He told her it was being decided right then whether Greece would still remain a member of the monetary union if the country failed to pay off its debts. He was trying to make conversation. She retorted that she didn't give a fuck about Greece, and that they were in debt, too. Then he blew a fuse. He roared, why the fuck does she always make it about herself, that is, about him? can't she look around and see what's going on in the world, what kind of pressure people live under and what kind of shit they have to take? She shouted him down, saying she had zero interest in other people's crap as she was suffocating in her own, and she demanded he tell her why he was constantly zombified in front of the TV since none of it concerned him at all! Why was he counting strikes in Spain? why was he calculating Romanian emigration quotas? why was he bothered about the amount of unpaid taxes in Italy? and why on earth did he have to convert into kilograms all the cash, diamonds and watches the former prime minister got for selling off this motherfucking country before he ended up behind bars? Why!!!?

To get some rest.

She didn't ask from what. Resolutely, she locked herself in the bathroom and left him alone with the wall. He wanted to smash it. She returned during the late-night news. The TV was back in place. Greece was approved for a new loan on the condition they implement austerity measures, at the expense of their citizens. She burst into tears. He said it was just her hormones, and she grabbed the red coat off the hanger and ran out. For the second time that night.

Where are you going!?

To Greece! To fucking hell!

He decided to wait for ten minutes and then go looking for her. In a little less than five, she was back. She looked like an earthquake, talking to her belly and pretending not to see him. He turned off the TV but it didn't help. He embraced her. Both her and the ball. He might have even said he was sorry. But she kept shaking and holding her belly in her hands as if she were indeed alone in the room, as if she were alone in the whole world, the world where everyone had their heads stuck in their own shit and their TVs, and there was no one to turn to for help, for support, for some understanding or a grain of optimism, because like they said on the news, and like he always claimed too, it will only get worse, and this in fact had nothing to do with her hormones. She kept saying: my poor child, while sobbing in his arms. It was his child, too, he reminded her. And indeed, it got worse. Both for her and for him.

The next day he found a message written in large letters on his car window: IDIOT. The handwriting was hers.

He assumes this little incident didn't escape the neighbour's attention either, which is why the neighbour talks to him as if he were indeed an idiot who'll silently agree with this diagnosis in the snow, and who'll swallow his banal sermon on peace, harmony and good intentions, as if he wouldn't get that it wasn't for the sake of the children on the other side of the kindergarten fence, but for his own child. But, to veer on the safe side, the neighbour doesn't tell him this directly, because he assumes the idiot intuitively feels he's an idiot, and that his tolerance must have its limits, too, and that his skin must get injured despite its thickness, and that there might already be a place on it worn thin by insults. That's why he rings the bell so early in the morning. He wants to ambush him. He's afraid he might hit him in that worn spot, and it could get awkward if he bleeds and blows his top, like he sometimes does, like a volcano – just like that time with Greece when he wanted to smash the wall, and just like now when he wants to hit the neighbour in the teeth with the man's own slipper and would prefer the neighbour not to speak to him in general terms and metaphors, but rather to hit him where he'll bleed: be it his child or his wife; not to beat around the bush with this complaint about disobeying the house rules and tarnishing the reputation of a once fine neighbourhood, but to openly tell him he's got serious family problems which are not only his, but problems for the whole building, if not the whole country, because his child is learning by bad example, and may – God forbid – grow up to be just like him, yet another emotionally handicapped and debt-ridden idiot, a burden to the community. Greece is full of such people.

Perhaps he's being overdramatic, perhaps the neighbour really thinks just what he says and is genuinely concerned about the rise in violence on their block and truly disturbed by the prospect of people digging through his own rubbish as well; perhaps this neighbour would never tell him what he wishes someone would finally tell him, even this early in the morning, so he could blow his top like all the decent people whose skin has worn thin. He'd like to be a decent man.

Surely she knows this, too?

He'd like to blow his top.

You can see it in his eyes. The neighbour can see it, too.

The neighbour backs away from the door and punches him lightly on the chest, like old buddies do, friends who understand each other with few words, the gesture almost an apology to show he fully understands his situation, with the child, with the wife, with the terribly tough times with no discernible end in sight, almost even justifying the fact that he sometimes needs a few more drinks to relax, that he sometimes has to raise his voice, if necessary as high as the third floor, where they clearly heard him the other day – it was Easter and they were slicing the boiled ham – and no one got angry, not at all, they were merely sorry that this dependable and conscientious man who helps others all the time doesn't seem to be able to help himself – and alas, he really can't.

The neighbour seems to know him through and through after all.

What did he want? she asks him later. It seems to her that they were standing at the door for an unusually long time. And he replies that the neighbour invited them over for coffee, would you believe, to socialise over coffee and cake; the neighbour said he'd really love them to come by and see his Easter decorations in the living room, especially her, since you can tell right away that she's an artistic soul who'll appreciate his work. Since he retired, he regularly designs such arrangements, is what he said, goes to the forest to collect moss, dry twigs and old stumps; and for Christmas he builds a nativity scene, with sheep and donkeys; and for Easter he makes bunnies and chickens, interspersing them with the figurines his wife makes out of bread: Mary, Jesus, Joseph, apostles, shepherds and kings, just like real ones. It would be nice to accept the invitation, he proposes, but she's reluctant. True, she's glad the neighbour saw in her what no one sees any more, and saw it right away, but Easter means nothing to her. She didn't even realise it had passed.

She'd only noticed the snow.

3

NO ONE KNOWS WHAT IT'S LIKE FOR HER. No one knows because no one bothers to ask, and this creates in her an unhealthy habit of confiding in objects, dirty dishes, wardrobe shelves, whatever's available, and so it's no wonder she feels misunderstood. This could make her ill, and that's the last thing she needs. That's probably why she's now climbing the stairs to the third floor. Slowly. She's put on a dress, put up her hair and applied lipstick. Her child is clinging onto a loose curl that was supposed to be dangling charmingly from her bun, the other hand trying to reach the light switches in the staircase. She whispers to be polite when they get to the neighbour's place, not to touch the switches there, not to stick any fingers in the sockets, not to pull on the tablecloth, not to open the drawers, not to get under the neighbour's feet, and so on, otherwise the neighbour will never invite them over again. Even though, truth be told, she doesn't really give a fuck about that, because Mummy hates Easter, she finds Jesus annoying, yet she has no better company, she says softly, and the child giggles into her ear, just like those dirty plates do, and the knickers in the wardrobe, as if understanding that she's uttered another of her contradictory statements. But she herself knows exactly what she means by it, since she's spent the whole day thinking about how stupid it would be to decline the coffee invitation and stay at home in front of the dumb wardrobe, trying to explain to it what she couldn't even explain to the neighbour – namely that Jesus is neither the first nor the last to have been abandoned by God, friends and fortune, just as he's neither the first nor the last to suffer unbearably, but he certainly was the only one who managed to profit from it, because, objectively speaking, there are countless others like him out there, abandoned and cruci-fied, biting the dust for the common good, a better future, or at least the future of their own children, waiting for mercy that's late or never coming, digging into their purses to find nothing but small change, and then they turn to God and ask him why he has robbed them, naively wondering why he's not respond-ing, as if they can't seem to come to terms with the fact that they're neither the first nor the last nor particularly original, and that suffering and empty wallets are a dime a dozen, and that their woes are as common as boredom, that the crosses on their backs are made of tin and plywood, whereas Jesus's cross is oak or marble and thus worth more. And they can bleed until the cows come home, still they won't earn sympathy, let alone get an Easter arrangement or their own little chapel. She could never explain this to him, you see, because the neighbour's heart is too small to have room for more than one Jesus.

Much like hers, really.

She won't buy into every complaint either; people simply like to whine, they like to overstate the dimensions of the crosses they bear so as to be taken seriously, and she can tell in a second if they're telling the truth or merely following the logic that a per-son just needs to be frustrated and penniless to seem honest. But she can immediately tell those who go on crazy weekend shop-ping sprees, from those who try to save up for the movies but then avoid the cinema altogether, ridden by guilt at the prospect of wasting money on such trifles, and she can just as easily assess the credibility of their problems by observing the shoes on their feet, the casualness with which they pay for parking or drinks, or by their inability to comprehend what she's actually saying when she declines to join them for lunch because a bread roll and a yogurt will relieve her hunger for a tenth of the price. That's why she gave up socialising. It was too expensive for her. And all that maths gave her a headache. Also, whenever they complained about things never having been so bad, she'd say she herself would never have it as good as they do and she'd be more than happy to swap her problems for theirs, she'd gladly suffer their stress, be constantly rushing to meetings, forwarding calls on her mobile phone and getting angry at being stuck in traffic, instead of spending her days in pointless arguments with furniture, trying to suppress the first symptoms of the mental illness that strikes anyone who has nothing to be late for. Her time is endless and cheap, but she should never admit it.

Now she knows.

Failure repels people.

Failure and small children.

Today she'll pretend she's doing well. Doing great, in fact. She'll prove it with her dress, lipstick and high heels, because fashion details tend to lift spirits much more than other people's compassion. Additionally, they divert attention away from the cross on her back. She'll play the woman who takes care of her spine and carries nothing heavier than flowers; she'll greet the hosts, express her admiration for the Easter arrangement and never let on that it took her forever to get to the third floor because she must have spent half an hour talking to herself. And the child has already lost interest in the light switches in the stairway. The baby yawns sleepily on her shoulder and waits for her to make a decision. Will she finally ring the neighbour's bell or return to the lower landing to gain a little more composure?

Be patient, she tells the child.

Mummy is nervous. Mummy's stomach churns like she's at a premiere. Mummy knows this anxiety too well, this fear of the audience, because she's an actress, it's her profession – her life plan had in fact been to concern herself with nothing more than flowers, her skin and accents, but then she was hit by a series of unforeseen events from which she never recovered, and which she keeps reconstructing and reliving in her head. And again she sees herself about to go on stage, repeating the lines that have scattered around her head in panic; she's cracking her knuckles, squeezing her bladder and saying blah blah blah to the mirrors, drawers and hangers in the theatre dressing room, never thinking that such conversations would become a habit; she's drawing out each sentence, buying time until she can recall the next one, which she then pulls out of her throat, one word at a time, as the stage manager's voice announces that the show is starting, the house is full – and he's already there, sitting in the second row, in the middle, she can't see him but he can see her, for the first time, just as everything is about to go wrong, just as she's getting tongue-tied and her knees start to shake – and she hates the job, and she hates the play, and she hates herself, and the last thing she needs is for someone to love her just as she is, at her worst, and he did it from the very start, loved her at her worst, applauded her with all his might, and later came over to her in the crowded lobby, only him, because only he couldn't see what everyone else saw, that she fucking sucked, but she won't think about the dangerous blindness of a man who looks but can't see, the dangerous man before whom you can shake, break down, collapse and still not be seen, and so she says yes to a drink, the first one and the fifth, she needs it, and he needs it too; for hours he keeps fumbling around her hands and knees, trying to be interesting, he talks of Dante and a couple of misfortunate

lovers enduring torment in the second circle of Hell, and she's
no idea how he arrived at the subject but she nods curiously and
confesses she's never read Dante, and that she's never heard anyone speak of horrors with so much passion, and it's already so
late, and he speaks less and less, staring at her smeared lipstick
and waiting for a sign, and she knows what he's waiting for; one
smile will be enough for their faces to finally collide, to grab at
each other's hair and clothes and fuck each other's brains out.
Then it's morning already.

And the series of unforeseen events keeps unfolding; she
pulls him close and can't let him go, for love is senseless and
tireless and won't be boxed up, placed under the pillow to wait
until the next day; she simply lost control, just as she will go
on to lose roles and miss boats, and it won't be long before she
starts claiming it's all his fault, that she's no longer the woman
she used to be, that no one is talking about her bright acting
future any more, and that they all avoid her like she's radio-
active. Love kills as soon as it gets a chance. And it's all because
of him – he was the one who irradiated her with his negative
energy, filled her head with statistics, depressing predictions and
paranoid scenarios, indeed it was he who explained to her the
secret pact between Jesus and the world order, in which there's
no room left for great roles; he was the one who, stubbornly
wanting to prove his point at all cost, went out into the icy car
park just now, without a jacket, to put the rubbish back in the
bin with his bare hands. Just to prove to her that things can
always get worse.

You wouldn't believe it, but they really can.

How many times has she told him this is all a product of his
shitty character? how many times has she warned him it can't go
on like this any more? how many times has she accused him of
just wallowing, wallowing, wallowing on that couch, like dust?
how many times has she caught herself uttering phrases she'd

rather have swallowed, still with no results, only for him to sink even deeper into the fabric of that same couch, ignoring even her sarcastic question of when he would finally die? Maybe she shouldn't say such things to him after all. Maybe all of this isn't his fault after all. It's this shitty government and Jesus who are to blame. They're the ones who fucked them over right from the start. She shouldn't have said that out loud, not in front of the neighbour and the others. That kind of language didn't suit her role or her hairstyle. It didn't suit the occasion either, because the song she heard from the other side of the neighbour's door sounded just like the one sung by the nuns clearing the snow. It died down when she rang the bell. Sitting inside there were people with disciplined kindness on their faces, dunking biscuits into coffee. The neighbour introduced her proudly, the lady here is an actress, he said, she has a husband with whom she moved into the building a year ago, but at the time she didn't have a child, only a belly that made her even more beautiful. They congratulated her, and she, quite certain the neighbour was embellishing, tried to divert their attention to something else, remarking on his creation that exuded the rotten smell of the forest. In the middle of the room, on a large carpet of moss, rose the stump of Golgotha with three stick crosses, dotted with pine cones and cypress twigs that probably represented palm trees. Next to it glinted the stable covered with leaves and fairy lights, whilst a tiny procession of bread figurines meandered between donkeys, cows and sheep towards a blue-painted egg laid in a wreath of dried mimosa flowers. The neighbour explained to her that the egg stood for Jesus' tomb, and she then conveyed this to the child. It's Jesus' tomb, we don't touch that. Then she complimented her neighbour for making everything look so real, even the bunnies peeking out from behind the cones. She tried to be likeable. The child cooperated, crawling politely around the arrangement, refraining from chewing anything. Good people observed her with curiosity. Oh, an actress? How wonderful. So, what is she in? Which theatre does she perform in? What play? Her voice seems familiar. They've got season tickets; costume dramas are their favourites. If you don't value history you can't value yourself either, right? And if you're not interested in drama, you can't have any interest in your neighbours, isn't that right? She was still staring at the construction. The bunnies had Dobermann muzzles. Just like those good people, in fact.

Then they switched to the first-person plural and started barking in unison.

We should protect our theatres instead of factories; a man can manage without a job, but not without spirit and tradition. There is work for anyone who wants to work, but we had to give our lives to defend spirit and tradition, so we'd never forget who we are and what we fought for, with God's help. It was for our history, not for bread, isn't that the truth? For our towns, tombs and borders that have defined us since time immemorial; not for the scum who never gave anything to this country and never buried anyone in this land. They've flocked here from all over. Even from China. No culture, no manners, no education, no respect for any real values; they barked away, their list of bullshit going on and on. The child was secretly crushing the mimosas around Jesus' egg, glancing in her direction and waiting for her reproach. It didn't come.

And what does her husband do? Surely he too is an artist?

Her husband?

He collects trash in the car park.

She blurted out the first thing that came to her mind. It flew out of her mouth with the speed of a thrown stone, shattering the chandelier and slamming into the glass cabinet. The effect was really quite similar. She took a slurp of her coffee in awkward silence. The neighbour laughed stupidly, and everyone thought she was joking. The child grabbed the egg and rolled it over the saints and domestic animals, and she did nothing to stop it; in fact, she felt like inflicting some damage herself, so she went on throwing stone after stone until she'd given answers to each question, in detail, starting with the fact that her husband did nothing, since his so-called education had not enabled him to do anything, he simply doesn't have the necessary qualifications, and the job market is awash with highly educated and well-bred people like him who seemingly don't want to work at all, even though they've spent half their lives learning Dante by heart, in the original, certain that this too would count as a job they'd be able to charge for; certain, indeed, that they're essential for the aforementioned struggle, as they'd know exactly how to put each person in their rightful place; dip some into boiling tar, let others be chased by hornets and wasps, have the third lot whipped with lizards' tails, drench the fourth with faeces, bind the fifth using ice; that's how they'd get rid of all the so-called scum, with poetry they could do it, and her husband could do it, his only legacy from reading Dante now being his contempt for people, especially those teeming with spirit and tradition, those who gave their lives for the same, those who think he's now indebted to them because of it, and above all, those like him, who obediently keep paying that debt back, selling all their books off and buying a cheap couch on which to wallow in depression, no longer caring about the contents of another person's soul, just the contents of their fridge, because souls can lie but the fridge, shoes or car never do, so claims her husband, and she agrees, because she too fell victim to the same damn historical struggle, but she didn't just lie there, she took up the first offer she got, and ever since then she's been shooting commercials for a supermarket chain, reciting idiotic lines about detergent, chocolate and chicken nuggets, and that's why her voice sounds familiar to them, that's where they know it from, but they failed to sense pathos in her interpretation, it never ever occurred to them that lines like those are only ever spoken out of desperation, she was sure they didn't give a rat's arse about drama, just like they didn't give a rat's arse about their neighbours; they listened to her reciting lines about discounts in the meat department and they went on consuming, consuming, consuming... They didn't applaud her when she was done.

She dropped the stone from her hand, grabbed the child, brushed moss off the little trousers, and carried the baby home. In one fist, the child was gripping a cracked blue egg, soon falling asleep with it. He, too, was already lying there, sewn to the couch. Carefully, she tore him from the upholstery and dragged him to bed. She lay him down half asleep, removed his trousers, kissed him on the cheek and lay her head on the pillow next to him. In the dim light he opened his eyes and saw her smiling at him. You stink, she whispered to him, but tenderly, as if wishing him a good night.

4

A THOUSAND YEARS AGO, MAYBE MORE, they got totally wasted. They sat on a beach littered with cigarette butts, fooling around, waiting for tourists to finally pack up their towels and scatter to their hotels, waiting for the sun to tumble over the horizon, the shore to blur into purple, the air to fill with cypress so they could take a good swig from the bottle, strip off all their clothes, jump into the sea, then jump each other's bones a bunch of times without contraception, and for life to take a completely different course. He laid out his shirt on the pebbles and lay her down next to him, and she pressed her backside into his lap, brought her lips up to his ear and whispered to him to be careful, for this is exactly how babies are made, mid-August, among the rocks, under a hunched cypress, on a man's shirt fashioned into a bed, as parents to-be are still dizzy from the sun, as the salty water gurgles against their eardrums, and alcohol makes them dumber than they already are, so they think there's nothing that can surprise them, not even tourists on a late walk along the shore. She distinctly remembers asking him to be careful, softly, as amiably as she could, not wanting to spoil the moment, and he let out a long shhhhh which was supposed to mean he'd got it all under control, and then he closed his eyes and eased himself into dizziness, certain there was nothing to worry about, because at that moment everything had to remain perfect. He also remembers making a fool of himself. He came almost immediately. He couldn't help himself. He tried to explain. It'd taken him by surprise. He hadn't expected it. It just came over him. Goddamn alcohol. He meant to apologise but she just waved it off, stood up and walked towards the sea. She washed her belly in the shallow water, observing him discreetly as he stood there bottomless, wordless, his knees scraped from the sharp pebbles, looking like an idiot, fumbling with his crotch and trying to understand the unfathomable; then she came back and sat down next to him, lit a cigarette and said something that sounded terrifying: what will be will be – it was succinct and absolutely precise, and he felt ice forming around his heart, along his spine, the worm between his legs shrivelled and suddenly the temperature dropped, it started to snow and summer ended with that one sentence, but he remained calm, he had no urge to run or cover his worm, it was a matter of honour; he put his arm around her shoulder, pulled her close and repeated those words, what will be will be, but brightly, with a lot of hope; he kept repeating them until they warmed up in his mouth, and so he laid them out like hot bricks in the shape of a house, and said it was their house which he'd build for her with his own hands, and heat with his own breath, and even though it didn't sound very convincing he was sure it would be warm and solid, and stand strong even after they'd sobered up. He talked a lot of nonsense, hoping she wouldn't remember it later, and made promises he didn't know how to fulfil; he said he'd give her everything he had, that is, the little he had, or even more precisely, everything that would be spent in the next few days.

Then he opened another bottle of wine. To celebrate.

A thousand years ago.

Perhaps even more.

Once there really was a summer, there were savings, there was sap flowing in the cypresses, and a setting sun, and purple beaches where they fucked each other's brains out and where a man's soul choked with emotion, liberated by the sight of sea and skin, liberated also by the wine he'd brought along and drunk on an empty stomach, making him say things he claimed he'd never said before, for instance that he could die of love, like in some great novel but right at the beginning, on the first pages, whilst the outcome of the story is still unpredictable, as he looked ahead and saw nothing but stars and the sparkle of the plankton, and everything shone before his eyes and he felt some kind of cosmic connection between his erections and the mysteries of nature; he said he'd never been so calm before, or so confused, but also never so scared by the realisation that the only thing that still made any sense in this cruel world was fucking, but this he also realised too late – he apologised for the words he used, he asked her if she believed in God in fate in horoscopes in numbers in the apocalypse in marriage, if she believed in the collapse of our civilisation and the global war of capital that will erase the little that's left of our tentative loves.

He did.

Especially when he was drunk.

She listened to him intently, scrunching her knickers in her hand and staring in the same direction he was, but much farther, across the glistening water towards the open sea, into black, and when he asked what she was looking at she said nothing, and when he asked what she was thinking about she said nothing, and when he asked what was going on with her, again she said nothing, and he was sure he understood this nothingness, when you think of nothing and when you need nothing, except maybe a cigarette, because you're just happy and you're trying to commit it to memory; he truly believed she was sitting there on that shitty beach without any desires, facing the darkness, relishing the uncertainty just like he did, and that she too felt like she could die, right then, while everything was still in place, undamaged, before they'd started resenting each other over promises unfulfilled, over weakness, laziness, selfishness, over stupid trifles and the goddamn rent, while they still believed that love saves, that love feeds, that love fixes what's broken, that love offers tacit answers to the most difficult questions and that it is, thank God, free. That's why he had hope and that's why he didn't throw himself off a cliff, that's why he didn't give in to the seductive tragedy of a great romance novel; instead, he repeated what will be will be, or rather, that it'd be all right, everything would be all right, everything would be all right, every single thing, and that was yet another small problem with love, that it lies like a tombstone.

He can't remember how they got to bed. He was drunk. He dreamt he was riding a bicycle. In the middle of winter. She was sitting on the handlebars, clutching on to them frantically, and she kept asking him to watch it, watch it, watch it, because the road was icy, the cars were speeding, and no one cared about cyclists. We'll crash! She screamed with all her might that they'd be crushed by oncoming vehicles, and he did indeed see a pair of headlights piercing the driving snow, so he made an abrupt turn towards the billboard on the left side of the road, rode right through it, and went on pedalling. He could hear his knees creaking and his teeth chattering and again she screamed careful, careful, as more cars sped at them, blinded by thick snow, so he turned right and went straight through a concrete wall, and he kept turning left and right, cycling through billboards, fences and walls, and just as he thought there was nothing to worry about because the world was built of jelly and air, they slammed into a brick wall, head on.

He woke up with his head throbbing right where he'd just hit the wall, whereas she lay on her back like a casualty, muttering never again and shielding her hungover face with her hands. She didn't speak to him. She kept her eyes closed and focused on the chemical processes in her ovaries. He tried to turn it into a joke. He took a pillow and stuck it under her nightdress, pressed his ear against it and pretended to listen for something to move; he tickled and caressed it, panting like a madman, and then he started pulling it out and, finally, held it up in the air and let out a whimper. She didn't find it funny. She kicked him in the stomach, turned on the other side and curled up like she was going to vomit. A few weeks later she did, for the first time. A few months later, something actually moved. It snowed. She bought a red coat with her maternity benefit money and started waking up an hour before dawn, submerged in black that once seemed miles away, and later, whenever he'd ask what was troubling her and what was on her mind, as always, she would say nothing.

She was lying.

Each morning she opens her eyes in the dark and waits for the room to grow bright. She hears the bells, she sees the silhouette of the child behind the cot slats, a ragdoll bunny and dirty laundry scattered across the floor; her face twists into a headachy grimace and she looks at the clock, always at the same time, then turns to him and tries to imagine life being different, she digs through the chapters in search of a point at which she could still have retreated, left a sentence unfinished or chosen some ambiguous conjunction, some but or still, and taken a turn into another story – and so she thinks back on that summer a thousand or so years ago, she can only vaguely recall the details, but she certainly remembers all the idiotic statements, like the one that only fucking can save them, but it's the glitch in her brain which he always reminds her of, that she only ever remembers the most idiotic sentences, only the most scathing criticism, only the worst performances, especially her own, and that she twists words until she detects their cruellest meaning, and that's why she needs someone to reinterpret everything for her, to tell her not everything is as black as it seems just now, before dawn; she needs someone who knows how to repair self-destructive machines like the one in her head, but that someone surely isn't him, which, to be fair, he freely admitted to her on several occasions, even when he made that idiotic remark about fucking, which meant that the only thing he knew how to do was blow his load on her stomach more or less in time, since it was the only way he knew of standing up to the world, the economic crisis, the waiting list at the job centre, the humiliating cash she would leave on the kitchen table, and which he wouldn't take immediately but only later, after he'd pulled on his boxers again feeling like he'd done something useful – but even that was getting harder and harder for him, this fucking for honour or for pocket money that he does without taking off his shirt and socks, as if he has chills and has to warm up his worm, blue with cold, and so he approaches her from behind, quietly apologising, as if asking for a favour she could easily refuse, because he wrongly presumes she'd rather be lying there in her own skin, alone and untouched; and then she feels like crying, it's hard to explain, maybe it's just another brain glitch that makes her see his consideration as offensive, and then she even mimics the same offensive behaviour, pulling down her knickers and telling him to be careful, that famous warning containing a whole scale of reproaching undertones, and it takes a huge effort on his part not to just give up, simply go to the kitchen and blow his load all over Page Three, where a warm-blooded woman offers her buttocks without additional cautioning; and it's quite certain they can't fuck like that for much longer, in misunderstanding, lying on their sides as he stares at the impenetrable back of her

36

head trying to figure out what she's thinking about while she's purportedly thinking about nothing, whilst she looks straight ahead, through tears, at the dirty laundry, at the ragdoll bunny, at the child sleeping in the cot, even though the baby would do her a big favour by waking up right now. There, that's what it's like to be in her head an hour before dawn, waiting for him to finally stir and possibly knock on her door and ask politely to come in; that's what's it like to hate him for the peaceful sleep that allows him to miss out on all the self-inflicted cruelties brought on by insomnia; that's what it's like to be completely oblivious to the fact that he's dreaming of crashing again, and he's rushing through the blizzard and through walls to save her, even if only in a dream; that's what it's like to live in delusion, to base life on the wrong assumptions, to be tormenting yourself without reason, to be torturing yourself from the early morning so you fail to notice the smile he shines on you when he sees you there next to him, in one piece, without a scratch, and he thinks how beautiful you are still, especially at this moment, before you open your mouth.

5

THE OCCUPATION IN THE CITY CENTRE BEGAN
AT NOON SHARP and he felt he should be there; he'd spent
a lot of time thinking about it, observing the processions of
poorly dressed men marching down the main street, whistling
and chanting: fellow citizens, join the peaceful protest of the
laid-off workers at such-and-such a factory – some would join,
some would cheer, and he would walk at the tail end of the procession alongside two or three police officers, until the march
scattered amid the trams and cars and other equally poorly
dressed people, or until it was simply dispersed by the rain. He
had time. He got drenched at the tail end of several similar processions, marches of the workers at the first, the second and the
tenth factory, he also visited the park where the hunger-striking
women from the eleventh factory set up camp, lying on blankets, knitting and playing cards, with their children visiting after school; once the national TV news crew van came, once and
never again, ambulance vans replaced it, some strikers ended up
in intensive care, others went back home, had a shower and a
square meal, maybe they managed to get by, maybe they didn't;
it's practically impossible to tend to the needs all of these miser-
able souls anyway, he thought, not meaning anything bad by it,

just trying to face the truth, to see himself in that mirror as well, because he too had wandered the city countless times with no money in his pocket, just as he went on a hunger strike countless times on the couch in the living room, with no strength to play with the crawling child – but she saw this as neither an act of rebellion nor of strike action, she didn't show him the slightest sympathy, she just accused him of slouching about, of leeching off her and not showing any results, she failed to realise that the goal of the protest is not to produce results but to maintain continuity, because when thousands of people sit in the street to stop traffic, protesting against politicians, judges, bankers or the corporate mafia who, ultimately, pull the strings of all their lives, and when they unfurl the banners that read ENOUGH, they know it won't be enough, just like the addressees of the message know it, and so the same scene gets replayed over and over again like in the theatre; but he gave up trying to explain to her how hard it is to take on the useless mission of sitting in, or of lying down and persevering, and instead he decided to go where he felt understood and do what can be done now that nothing can be done, at noon sharp – and so he took an empty box of baby formula, unfolded it into a rectangle, and on the inside of the cardboard with a ballpoint pen he wrote CROOKS.

He retraced the lines of the letters several times and added an exclamation mark. He did this covertly, then stuffed the cardboard under his jacket and told her he had to go out, there was something he had to do, catching her on the verge of a nervous breakdown while she was scraping burnt milk off the bottom of a pot, with the pee-soaked child trying to climb her leg, while she was begging the baby to wait, to wait for just one second, all the while trying with enormous difficulty to refrain from screaming or breaking something, because the child was bawling angrily and slapping at her thigh with tiny hands, demanding the right that every child should be able to claim, not to have to wait, just as he demanded the right that every man should be able to claim to pursue goals more noble than washing the dishes and wiping up urine. Without having to explain himself.

I won't be long, he said and ran out into the stairwell. The neighbour walked past him as though he didn't see him. It might have been unintentional.

And so, at noon sharp, he stood among a few hundred people, listening to the speech aimed at the city authorities. The young man behind the megaphone explained to the crowd why they were protesting. He reminded them that not so long ago, on the square where they now stood, there was a historic building that the city government hadn't known what to do with, so in the shady process of selling off public space, they handed it over to a private investor who brought in excavators and razed history to the ground, putting up a shopping mall with mirrored windows in its place. But when it turned out that the newly opened shops were getting no business, the investor decided to lure in consumers by building a multi-storey car park that would make it easier to access the shops. The pedestrian zone surrounding the glass monument to corruption happened to be an ideal place for this new private investment. The young man behind the megaphone chose his words carefully. After a series of corruption scandals and unfinished city projects funnelling millions in public money into the pockets of somebody's uncles and cousins, the city government had flouted the law once again, excluding the citizens from the decision-making process and enabling a private individual to enrich himself unscrupulously by seizing something that belonged to everyone. The pavement.

He held his sign high up in the air.

Crooks!

The young man called for a joint act of civil disobedience to express their disapproval of the city's barbaric appropriation; he invited them to surround the steel hoarding that guarded the hole gaping in the middle of the pedestrian zone and to knock it down with their own hands. The crowd began reshuffling, and he found himself facing the blue hoarding panels supported by stabilisers inside the perimeter. Through the crack between two panels, he caught sight of the worried face of a security guard. He laid his hand on the frosty panel and waited for the others to strike.

The fence shook.

Once, twice, then he joined in.

A rhythm of collective beating was now established, rocking the fence at steady intervals as the joints between the metal supports rattled with vibrations. It sounded like a symphony. The security guard on the other side of the panel was trying his best to keep the hoarding upright, supporting it with his shoulder. His face was only six inches away, crimson from straining, and pressed into the crack so that the edge of the metal panel cut into his cheek. Whenever he slammed on the panel, he'd effectively slap the guard as the supports trembled; he didn't mean to, his hand hurt and he honestly hoped the guy wouldn't take it personally, because he was really only slapping him in the common interest, like a peaceful and honourable man who loathes violence, a man who'd never hit a woman or a child or a neighbour, in spite of his empty threats that he'd do it one day, his wife first, knock her against the wall as she screams the same sentence for the tenth time, then walk over to the cot and shake the child who is hysterically howling despite being neither hungry, wet or cold, and then open the door for the neighbour, come to complain about the noise, and punch his lights out with a professional uppercut, catapulting him back to his living room on the third floor; it's true, he had threatened to do this, but he never actually did it, for the simple reason of being able to draw the distinction between words and deeds, just as he was now able to distinguish the symbolic act aimed against a certain group of people, from the concrete slap delivered to someone else, counting on everyone seeing the metaphorical shortcut between the construction site in that square and the crooks on his sign, and therefore he couldn't be held responsible if, in the rhetorical entanglement of this complex situation, an innocent cheek found itself at the scene of a crime.

He is capable of discerning these nuances but he's not quite sure if the security guards understand them too, because it could be that they're not protecting the construction site at all, but rather their high-stress, low-paid jobs. He assumed that's how it was in the war, too, the one of twenty years ago, when real people were suddenly wearing skins of symbolic uniforms and when some symbolic country was suddenly on someone's real piece of land, creating such confusion that no one could tell where reality began and rhetoric ended, nor where attack began and self-defence ended. He could clearly remember foreign TV news commentators trying to figure out what exactly was going on in that war, who was with whom, who was against whom, and why; but they never came up with anything particularly clever except that it was a tribal conflict where people put up barricades and slaughtered each other in hand-to-hand combat over roads, bridges and meadows, and thus, naturally, they failed to see the metaphorical character of the problem, which is that both the people and the country were collateral victims of incompatible rhetorical constructions, that they were all branded with symbols like bulls, so when people shot at each other they were actually aiming for the brand, not the head. And since the expert analysis didn't concern itself with symbolism but merely with strategic moves, no one could raise the alarm about the inevitable consequences, and no one could see that reaching symbolic goals would bring only symbolic victories, so that each battle for a road, bridge or meadow would become fundamentally meaningless, because the prospective winners would get nothing but nominal rights and spectacular ceremonies on the new national holiday, but this would become clear only later, through the examples of pedestrian zones and multi-storey car parks, this fact that the fight had been merely rhetorical, that it had taken place on the surface, on the skin, in language, while the real ownership of maps and floor plans was arranged in more peaceable circumstances, in secret meetings where sales contracts were signed, bribes were distributed and cash was counted over shots of single malt, marking a spectacular triumph of numbers over blood and words.

The fence toppled.

A victorious hurrah reverberated through the mass of protesters. There was a sound of whistles and rattles, then the Internationale was heard from somebody's phone, and a few girls climbed on the collapsed panels and started bouncing on them joyfully. The fence lay on its back. The girls stomped on its belly. And in the midst of it all, huddled around a muddy hole in the ground stood the security guards, the wretched of the earth. The one he'd been slapping until a moment ago was looking straight at him. The guard could have been his father. He had the familiar expression of bewilderment that marked the faces of the fathers of his generation, the disabled and other war veterans who suddenly found themselves on the wrong side, though they'd done nothing but follow orders, and so they couldn't fathom how all this had come about, this wretched inversion; why, having only ever done their duty, done their job honestly, the only thing they had to show for it were skeletons and debts.

He had a feeling the guard might be one of those cases, with PTSD and shrapnel in his buttocks – he might have a wife who could never give him comfort, as she herself had gone mute with shock, worry and uncertainty, then guilted him with her silence, and even though she'd always thought she'd leave, she never did, she gave him a child and turned into a beast – but the child left home as soon as they could, ran for their life and enrolled at college so they wouldn't end up like their father, who still keeps waiting for the child to call and ask him how he's doing, if everything's all right, even though he knows the child isn't really interested in the answer, and they won't call, because the child doesn't give a fuck about their father and his integrity, because the child can't bear to listen to the same rant about there being no justice in the world, which he'd been repeating since forever in various contexts; when he left for Germany to work in construction at the age of twenty and learned that work can be shameful; when he spent the last dime of his savings at the age of thirty and realised he should never have gone back; when he lay in a ditch in some ruinous rural back of beyond at the age of forty, as mortar rounds sifted the ground around his feet; and at the age of fifty when he finally realised that all this hadn't made him a hero in the eyes of others, but an idiot; and now because he's already sixty and hasn't yet paid off the mortgage on his tiny flat in the suburbs, from his low-paying job which he'll most likely lose that day – so when he thinks again that there's no justice, he's actually giving the correct, albeit well-worn diagnosis of the situation, because for him there's no justice on either side of the fence, just as there was never justice on either side of the barricades; and he could probably stomach those girls' shoes recklessly trampling the last line of defence that he failed to protect, he could tolerate the cynical whistles celebrating yet another defeat he won't get paid for, he could even endure that stupid commie song that talks about him far more than any of them, he could perhaps take many more real and symbolic slaps and never hit back, but when a person points a sign at him calling him a crook for everyone to see, a crook with an exclamation mark no less, someone who could well be his son, that's where he draws the line and strikes back with all

45

his might – he grabs the sign-wielder by the jacket, grips his throat, snatches the cardboard away from him and rips it into pieces, spits in his face, and as someone's hands are pulling him away so he doesn't kill this man, he's still yelling: you ungrateful piece of shit, you should be ashamed of yourself!

Me?

He reckons this is what it was like in the war, too.

Those you fight for despise you the most.

Your own people will always hurt you most deeply.

That's why, after all of this, the hardest thing is coming home. She asks you where you've been, what you did and what it was good for. She knows exactly where it hurts most, and she'll stab you in that very spot, all the while holding the kitchen knife as if by accident. She sits at the table over two empty plates, shredding a paper napkin with the knife, and by the way she looks at you it's clear you've stayed out way too long, because she's already scrubbed that pot clean, she's changed the child and washed the little pyjamas, and the child has already eaten up the baby food and scattered building blocks around the room, and after a whole day of playing in which your presence was not missed, the child went to sleep, and she rocked the little body in her arms until they went numb, and she told a story about the snowman that melted in the convent yard across the street; the child didn't understand the words but still fell asleep distressed, and then she tiptoed out of the room, filled up a bucket of water and scraped the remains of the mud off the floorboards – she scrubbed the bathroom and the kitchen, she polished the miniature handprints off the windows and set the table, she even lit a candle and warmed up the dinner, and then went on shredding minutes into milliseconds with a knife, and even though she could have called you, she didn't, just as you could have called but you didn't, because you needed time to pull yourself together, to wash your face, for Christ's sake; but none of this

46

really matters now as you stand before her blade, inhaling the smell of cleaning products, observing the obsessive tidiness with which she tirelessly maintains all the surfaces, and it strikes you that you might indeed have ruined this woman's life, and spine, and nails, definitely her day, but you've no strength to talk about it, just like you've no strength to eat, and she might as well blow out the candle and dump the rest in the rubbish, feeling like a dumb cow, that's right, and you apologise in vain, in vain you tell her you'll sleep on the couch, in vain you promise you'll explain everything tomorrow... you won't.

6

IT'S NOT THE FIRST TIME he's taken the bedding over to the couch to crawl under the duvet as if at gunpoint, it's not the first time she's asked him why he doesn't leave, humiliating him with the fact that he's got nowhere to go, and it's not the first time she's forced him to admit things he otherwise lacks the courage to say; how much he hates coming home, how hard it is to drag his feet up the stairs and unlock the door, his stomach tied up in knots, nauseously walking down the hallway, anxiously looking around the apartment for her body among the furniture because he expects to see her there, hanged, poisoned or slashed, with a sneaky message left on the kitchen counter explaining she's done him a favour. It's not the first time he hasn't had the strength to defend himself, so he just keeps repeating it's not like that, it's not like that at all, and he hangs his head between his shoulders like a man in mortal danger, helplessly blinking the eye that's peeking out from under the quilt, saliva dripping from the corner of his mouth, without a sentence to sop it up. It's not the first time he's been lost for words at a decisive moment, it's not the first, although he always tells himself it's the last time – he rams his face into the saliva-sodden pillow and recites Dante to himself; by the time he's reached the middle of a canto she's usually gone, given up, and he can sometimes hear her whimpering in the bedroom and talking to herself, as he falls asleep cycling down a snow-swept street towards the first intersection where he'll turn neither left nor right; he'll just pedal on, straight into the first car he sees, and send it all to hell.

In the morning he'll pack up his things.

He'll be doing her a favour.

That won't be a first either, and it won't surprise her, as he's already threatened to leave and then decided to come back on several occasions, like that time back then – over some bullshit – he can't even remember what it was any more – except that it took him less than ten minutes to pack up everything he owned. A few shirts and sweaters, a pair of trousers, a plastic bag of pants and socks, a toiletry bag and a phone charger. He threw his backpack on and walked out. Just like that. The shoes he'd worn at their wedding, he forgot in the hallway. And although she herself had told him it was best that he pack up and piss off, at the door she accused him of taking the easy way out. She expected this obviously flawed logic to stop him in his tracks, and for him to cling on to her garbled phrases as proof that everything she'd been saying was total nonsense. She was ready to admit she hadn't meant it like that, and to agree it made no sense to do anything rash now, and to repent – granted, under her breath, but audibly enough for him to accept the apology and tell her he loved her, in spite of everything, for better or worse, as he'd once stated before witnesses.

The shoes left on the floor might have reminded him of the promise, she believed they would, but he took the whole thing quite literally and dashed out the door as if escaping a fire, grazing her shoulder with his backpack on the way out. She heard him skipping steps and opening the stairwell door; a few seconds later the engine roared in the car park, and then everything was as before, only motionless. She didn't make a scene, not right away; he might still be back knocking at the door before she'd counted to a hundred. She put his shoes away, prepared a baby bottle, then crouched by the crib and counted, one, and two, and three, and then one hundred, and two hundred – and when she passed three hundred, she felt like a fool; numbers just flew by without any control, buzzing around the room like flies, slamming into everything. One landed on her cheek. She slapped it down hard, and the child woke up. She whispered, my little bunny my pet my teddy bear, kissing the child's snout, tail and paws, and then she fed the baby, changed the little outfit, laid the downy head on her shoulder and marched from wall to wall, a mile, until the child was asleep again. Her cheek hung from her face like a rag all the while. She went to the bathroom and pulled it up back into place. That's how it came to pass back then – over some bullshit.

For the next few hours she could focus on herself exclusively, start a new life before the child woke up again, call a security company and have the locks changed, ask a neighbour to lug that couch down to the basement, and start over, just as she had threatened to do many times before, just as she should have done long ago, while she had a crystal-clear reason to do it, but she pretended she had more important things to do, poking around the surface of the mess, moving objects a little to the right or a little to the left, picking crumbs off the table with her index finger, opening drawers and closing them again, rummaging through packaged items in the cupboards and checking their expiration dates, wasting time on rubbish, pretending nothing had happened, that he'd merely gone to the shops and got stuck in traffic. Her vision fogged up; but no, those weren't tears, just finely printed dates on the packaging making her eyes water.

The 26th of January of this year.

She remembered it all.

She also recognised the wine bottle shoved deep into the back corner of the kitchen cupboard. He'd brought the wine to the hospital to celebrate the birth of the child, planting it on the nightstand. She asked him not to embarrass them. He asked her why she was whispering. She told him he could have brought flowers. Again, he said he couldn't hear her and bent his head down towards her. She was silent.

Why are you being like this?

Because of the roses.

He didn't understand. He was drunk. He swayed over her bed for a while, waiting for a better explanation, then took a snapshot of the baby with his mobile, picked up the bottle and left. On the way out, he scolded her for always ruining everything; he said he was fucking sick of this state of emergency, but that he'd save the wine for them to drink together once her postnatal depression had lifted. She shook the bottle now. It was empty.

She tossed the damn shoes in the bin, shoving the bottle in there too, and then proceeded to kill time with geometry. She adjusted all the blinds to the same height; she arranged old magazines chronologically, stacking them neatly; she positioned the chairs at equal distance then tucked them under the table; she crawled into the chair opposite his, and – in a touching soliloquy that she could never reproduce – she explained that she was a good and diligent woman who was simply going through a complicated phase and thus had the right to lose her shit over little things, such as wine, such as flowers, and even to say some really nasty things from time to time, and not be taken seriously, and that she had every right to ask him where he'd been, who he'd been with and what he was doing, and whether he still loved her as much as she loved him. More than anything in the world.

The chair across from her was silent.

Her vision fogged up again, but it must have been the smoke. She hadn't smoked since the start of her pregnancy, though he assured her that was just as harmful, since abstinence made her insufferable, contradictory and full of self-pity, and it was only a matter of time before she'd start bingeing on high-calorie junk and her own cuticles; to this she retorted that she was neither edgy nor hungry, not at all, not in the least, except when he insisted otherwise; she chewed gum, blew sticky bubbles and took it out on obscene amounts of lettuce, and only when she told him to leave that morning, only to then reproach him for leaving, only then did she feel a strong urge to binge; she stuck her fingers between her teeth and bit her nails, and she had to admit he'd been right when he made the diagnostic distinction between real hunger and a mental disorder. She smoked until she was sated. At 5 p.m. she began to cough. Late in the evening she felt the smoker's fear.

Each cigarette steals approximately seven minutes of your life.

She's already lost a whole hour in a single afternoon.

She's...

She switched off her brain at the start of the sentence, forbade it to keep working, then turned on all the lights and forced herself to think of nothing but furniture and accumulated dust. Then she fished the shoes out of the bin, dumped the contents of the ashtray in them, and put them back in the hallway so that one day, eventually, when he walked through that door again, they would remind him of the responsibility he bore for her untimely death – and so she sat by the window and waited and waited and waited to say it all to his face, until the very last car returned to the car park and she fell asleep in her seat, for a few seconds, and then was startled awake as her forehead slammed against the window sill, the image in front of the building still exactly the same, frozen and motionless, and any fool could see it was better to go to bed than to keep running up the electricity bill. She put a band-aid on her forehead, emptied the ash out of the shoes, sprayed them with air freshener, put on her night-dress, and then returned to the same spot and sat and sat and sat until her eyes started burning and life lost all meaning, and only then did she send everything to hell and switch her brain back on, turn it up to max and let it do what it would with her. She expected to have a good cry at last. But she didn't.

The tears just wouldn't come.

Not a single one.

These things happen: women walk a mile between walls, lose a whole night over some bullshit, put superhuman effort into it, and then, instead of breaking down, surrendering and finally resting, they stay bolt upright, as if they'd swallowed a broom or simply turned to stone. They even manage to wear clean clothes. Whereas men fall apart right away, they shatter like glass, no longer serving any purpose – yet it's not their fault, they're merely reacting honestly. Men are confused by the sight of those wrinkly bunnies, pets and teddy bears falling out of red maternity coats and calling themselves their children; men are startled by the thought of a difficult sleep-deprived phase in which they'll have to start loving those children, as well as the realisation that the miracle of birth passed them by as they took part in it only technically, since they experienced no pain or suffering – and so they retreat at the accusation that they don't understand anything, that they don't understand anything at all, which she said to him several times that morning, and instead of realising it was just a symptom of dramatic mood swings for which she had medical justification, he took it all quite liter-ally, skipped the debate, skipped steps on the dash downstairs, and left without a word. And all that just to demonstrate to her, sourly, that he was not needed at all because, at the end of the day, every baby manual claimed the child needed only the mother, the breast and milk; each baby manual omitted his role, although she had done her best to assign him the worst one, way back there in the maternity ward, when they were told the child was too weak to suckle, had been born tired and listless, lacked the survival instinct – in short, that the child took after him.

She gave the diagnosis herself.

She stayed at the ward for five full days, with a nurse on duty by her bedside, patting the baby on the bum, tickling tiny cheeks and pulling dinky ears to wake the child up; the nurse would then tug her breast out of her gaping nightdress for her and squeeze it hard, extruding the nipple with her fingers, spraying milk across the drowsy child's face, and then she'd push the baby against her chest, firmly holding its head. The baby's shoulders would tremble from crying, slowly starting to go purple. On the fifth day they gave up. She was instructed to bottle feed the baby, and to squeeze out the excess milk down the drain. But that was not an easy job either, squeezing out litres of baby feed through the fine sieve of her nipples, and furthermore, something in there was clogged. Her breasts swelled, her skin cracked, she got a fever and had to return to the hospital, fearing she might explode. They gave her a shot and sliced her open with a scalpel at heart level. They poured the milk out into a bucket and sent it out for analysis, and they wrapped her in multiple layers of gauze and told her to go home, assuring her all she had to do was to change the bandage regularly and disinfect the wound, which would heal on its own.

It's nothing, they told her.

It's nothing, she echoed to him, assuming he saw the irony.

He should have known that everything he'd do would be wrong. Even back then. A newspaper had published statistics saying that one in three marriages was doomed. It cited housing instability, social insecurity, alcoholism and unequal division of household chores as reasons, and stated that a significant percentage of relationships broke up after the birth of the first child, in the middle of the night, as the crying bunnies, pets and teddy bears sounded the alarm with no one there to comfort them, because the parents had closed all the doors to the kitchen, where they were grabbing each other's throats over a table engulfed in cigarette smoke, holding each other to blame for not being happy.

They have it so easy, don't they? the neighbours said, what with not having to go to work in the morning. But he didn't give a rat's arse about the neighbours' opinions; he just wanted to know who was to blame. Because when he bolted out the door and started the car, he really wasn't sure why he was doing it – maybe he wanted to prove to her that the void he was leaving wouldn't be insignificant; maybe he wanted her to miss him after all, sometime around 2 a.m., when she'd have to face the fact that the shops had long closed and the roads were now clear; maybe he was counting on a passionate reconciliation ensuing after she'd called him a bunch of times; or maybe, to be completely honest, he just jumped at this opportunity to get a decent night's sleep at last. He sped out of the car park, drove a semi-circle around the apartment block and turned into a muddy dirt road leading into the patch of trees that stretched along the fence behind the convent. He turned on the radio, put his seat all the way down, and fell asleep. He woke up around 8 p.m. in complete darkness, chilled to the bone and stiff, with a strong urge to be the first to give in. He got out of the car, had a piss, and walked about fifty yards towards the convent fence to where he could see the lights of their windows. Even if she was standing there, she couldn't see the man amid the branches, in the black patch of trees, trying to type a message of penance on his mobile phone with a numbed thumb. The message slowly made its way through the thick winter air and arrived within reach of her lit windows, only to be rerouted back by the mobile company with the note that there was not enough credit on his account to complete the request. He got back into the car. He felt a sudden urge to start the engine, step on the gas, tear from the dirt road straight into the main road, crashing into the first pole, the car rolling and landing on its roof; and just before he lost consciousness, he would dictate her phone number to the ambulance paramedic. In this, at least, there would be some dignity. It then crossed his mind that he could drive downtown, find some company and get shitfaced, playing the euphoric father, and end up under the table so they'd have to take him home and deliver him, crawling on all fours, to his wife. No one would blame him. He counted the money in his wallet. He didn't have enough for more than one round. Then he clambered over to the back seat, buttoned his jacket up to his chin, and with the nagging feeling of doing the wrong thing again, he went back to sleep. At 5 a.m. he was at the door. He could hear the shower running from the hallway. He put down his backpack and crept to the bathroom. She was standing there, leaning over the tub, water trickling down her hair. She looked like a polar bear under a waterfall. The loose skin of her belly spilled over the top of her knickers, and her breasts were still wrapped in bandages. He coughed to get her attention and she turned off the tap, asked him not to look at her, and covered herself with a towel. He turned his head away. Then she told him she hated him.

He said he knew that.

That she really hated him.

He knew that too.

From the bottom of her heart.

He believed that.

Then they embraced.

If he were writing this novel, that is, if he had money and a room of his own, and her wholehearted support for his writing, he would end the story with this scene. He would describe a bear raised on her hind legs, laying her paws down on her mate and leaning on his majestic shoulders in a wrestler's grip, and him, a one-ton monstrosity, opening his jaws wide and sticking out his tongue to lick the wet fur on her neck. It would be a novel with a happy ending, resolving in its grand finale the paradoxical relationship between words and embraces; he wouldn't even mention anything beyond, he would steer clear of the future, with its many neck pains collected on the couch and numerous deaths at a snow-swept intersection, or being woken by a child screaming, and her dark gaze staring at the dead man lying in his place, and her acerbic question conveying so clearly that it's harder to survive a morning than a car crash.

You're still here?

She's holding the tear-soaked pillowcase in her hand, then she lays it over the radiator and walks stiffly over to the kitchen, where she proceeds to bang plates, pots and kitchen cabinet doors, while the child follows her example, grabbing a toy, hitting it against the door frame and having a breakdown when the toy falls apart at the fifth swing. You're just like your father, she says, destroying everything you lay your hands on; then she snatches the broken pieces of plastic from the child's hands, throws them in the bin and continues demolishing the kitchen, reassuring herself that she hasn't always been a monster. And she's probably sorry; she probably would really like to hug the child, fix the toy, take off her monstrous skin, then go back to bed and try to wake up again and wish him good morning without sarcasm. If he were writing this novel, she would probably do all that, but he doesn't have money, nor a room of his own, nor her wholehearted support; he always has to have someone to blame.

7

GO AHEAD, WRITE, WRITE, WRITE, she tells him, as if it were the easiest thing in the world, as if you could just sit down and start writing, for instance that sentence from a minute ago, about two bears banging on the bathroom floor, without it sounding moronic. She thinks writing is like fishing; you cast your line and wait, you're bound to catch something – and so she says write, just like that, and she'll close the door and tiptoe so as not to scare the fish, or better yet, she'll take the child out to the park, wrapped in a blanket, go out into the knee-deep slush, all so he can catch a specimen, so that he can WRITE in peace, instead of pecking endlessly at the same single sentence, struggling with the bear couple who've been locked in a clinch for days now, holding on and not letting go, so that it's not clear if they're about to fuck or slay each other, just as it's not clear why they're doing this in the first place; he himself doesn't have a clue what the bear did to his mate to make her hate him so much, nor what the she-bear did to the he-bear to make him want to smack her in the gob. And yet she still tells him go on, write, don't give up, change the subject, try again, as if writing redeems, as if it'll compensate for all the negligence and laziness he likes to call fatigue; all the days he slobbered away on the couch watching live parliamentary sessions and listening to them tell him from the podium that it's time to tighten his belt, or take out a loan, the top-up kind, for bread, milk and phone bills, because everything that could be looted has been looted and everything that could be sold has been sold, and all the money is now gone unless someone lends him some; and so they warn him to be careful with that, too, because other people's money is easily spent and hard to pay back, as they know best, and they advise him to just hold on for another twenty or thirty years until the appropriated assets are returned to the people in dividends, and to just keep his worm in his pants and not make babies in the middle of a recession, for which, of course, it's too late now, so they laugh at him with good reason – he's ended up looking like a fool, earning every right to bang his head against the wall, as if banging his head against the wall was his only right, the only justified response, the only thing he could ever be good at, and presumably that's why she keeps telling him to sit down and write, to mind his head and do what he's missing out on every day, a miracle no less; to do something beautiful and noble with words, instead of smearing them on the floor like spit. And she truly believes in this sacred undertaking of his; she gently squeezes his hand and tells him only writing can save them, and she takes the blanket and the child and walks out into the slush, and as she slips out of his sight around the corner it seems to him that miracles are indeed possible, because she's walking above the ground and her feet aren't touching that shit on the road at all. And so he starts to write, just like she told him to, from the beginning, from a blank slate, and he imagines a novel that could easily be this novel because he would also call it *Love Novel*, and he would also set it in a similar sold-out place miles from anywhere where people walk backwards or on all fours, with their heads banged up and their worms squeezed between their legs, digging through the rubbish and growling at one other over a worn-out maternity coat, where man is bear to man, figuratively speaking; he'd write it as if he had nothing left to lose, as if he'd get gastritis or a stomach ulcer if he didn't, as if it would bring relief, only to be unpleasantly surprised because the words would spin him in a circle, rebutting each other by some logic of their own, delaying the happy ending and forcing him to keep going even when he didn't want to anymore, to write like he lives, without a plan, from one day to the next, not knowing what will happen on the next page when, for example, she comes back from her walk, chilled to the bone, and reads the sentence she's already heard and didn't like, and which, perhaps, she was the one to have uttered, and then she realises he lacks the imagination to invent a better story than this pitiful one that's theirs, which, if he'd really like to know, literature doesn't need at all, especially not now when people are craving books to bring them comfort and hope, books that, in her words, bring salvation; and not this defeatist crap where everything is already lost and doomed, and which, she'd like to add, has nothing to do with love, because love is sex, love is longing, love is bubbles, flowers, chocolate and the smell of cinnamon, love is an unspeakable ecstasy that defies gravity, recession and life's blows, and lifts us above the slush on the road and the mud on the floor, and for which he, unlike her, doesn't have a shred of talent. But he still wants to write this very novel, although it's clear as day to him that he won't, because the mere thought of all the artistic affectations, the crises, the blocks and the huge amounts of alcohol he'd have to invest in makes him sick to his stomach, much like the assumption that no one would actually read his stuff; at the same time, he fears the picture in which he can see himself if he got all that voltage out of his head; if he vented it all out, if he came clean, if he reached the chapter in which he's presumed to be writing or, like, fishing; watching the float lazily inch across the white

surface, rolling himself a cigarette, his thoughts constantly re-
verting to the face of the waitress who happened to be on the
other side of the bar when he fled the underground car park
construction site, all dishevelled and spat upon, and in a trem-
bling voice ordered a double shot of Pelinkovac, when he needed something to calm him down, when he needed to wash his
face and get wasted, because a minute earlier, let's not forget,
that man had tried to strangle him; and so he rolled the empty
glass between his fingers and kept saying fuck this revolution,
fuck these people, fuck the state, not expecting her to hear him
at all, let alone understand him, or least of all to refill his glass,
sit next to him and say something no one's said to him for cen-
turies – that he's right, that he's got every right to curse everything under the sun because she does it too, every time she asks
herself why she's waiting tables instead of studying, why she's
slinging beers instead of taking exams, or erecting barricades,
because yes, that also crossed her mind when she thought about
this shithole country where the most she could hope for was to
put on rubber gloves and dive into shit up to her elbows, wash
glasses, make coffee, clean floors, and try to keep her spine
straight and not let every other bastard grope her arse as she's
emptying ashtrays. But he can't write about it because it would
make him look like the same kind of bastard, it would seem like
he exploited the situation just to get a piece of that arse, although now, truth be told, he can't even remember the name of
its owner, which is completely understandable, at least to him,
because he was out of his mind and couldn't control his head,
his hands or the words that sprang out of his Pelinkovac, splash-
ing like dolphins and breaking their necks on the bar; but suddenly it felt great to be so drunk and so stupid, he wanted to
make a toast to getting out of it all alive, aliiiiiive, a toast to
sitting across from a woman who's not rolling her eyes at him,
who's not dismissing him with a wave and a bah, and who's not

staring at him the way he stared at parliamentary sessions, annoyed in advance by what they had to say to him; so he solemnly raised his glass and announced that all was not lost, that everyone should look at the bright side of life, especially her, because she had no loans, or kids, and would still be young and beautiful even in those twenty or thirty years when the unsustainable greed of capital finally devoured itself, and things were looking up, which, of course, was a stale phrase, but she seemed to like it nevertheless, because she said cheers, and she poured him another one, and smiled at him again, and then she kept saying that they must have met before, she must have seen him somewhere before, in the newspapers or even on TV, which could only be explained by the fact that guys like him were a dime a dozen, and that every drunk resembled another drunk and it's easy to mix them up, mirroring each other's gestures, curses, bad poetry and speculative theories, like the one on the afterlife which he advanced to prove to her that there was a secret connection between their destinies, drooling into her ear as he analysed the constellations of their souls in past lives, claiming their paths had crossed even back then, that they had most likely been rivals or enemies, on opposite sides of the barricades, perishing in wars and duels, only to find themselves on the same side after much wandering, behind the masks, tragically miscast, and now they were being given a chance that they'd either seize or blow.

And even though this was utter bullshit, again she said he could be right, and why not? – as if she was really glad their paths had crossed again, and she was willing to put her arse on the line, figuring it was better to take what she could get right now than wait for what's not going to come later; because that's what she's destined for, after all, and he's neither the first nor the last with a wife and child and dinner waiting at home, and there was nothing special, unforgettable, let alone everlasting she could hope for with him, so she could give him tacit permission to do whatever he wanted with her, no strings attached, unbutton her bra and take off her jeans after she's come off her shift, and call her wonderful, smooth, dazzling or something like that, only to take it all back with an uninspired explanation that he hadn't known what he was doing, that he couldn't remember where he'd parked his car, or where he'd left his skin, nor how he would ever squeeze back into it, let alone how he would pay the bill and get back home, and he didn't think he should have to justify himself, which he surely would not, because the truth is he was drunk and he truly saw those dolphins, and collapsed over the bar together with them, and then reared up onto his elbows again, soft and unscathed – and that's why it seemed to him that he could do all the things he usually couldn't, like talk bullshit, drink on credit, lose track of time, and that's why he felt he had the courage he otherwise lacked, and the inspiration he was lacking right now, felt he could fly or write, that is that he wouldn't actually even need to, because he already had the whole novel in his head; with the neighbour, the child, Jesus, Dante, the bears, and the next few decades in which he would make love solely out of panic, and all that had to be done was to store it away safely and unpack it somewhere quiet, and then effortlessly catch all the fish jumping out of the package, which are now swimming on the ceilings and walls, silent and out of his reach.

But again he has no words to describe this state.

He doesn't have enough alcohol to escape it either.

And besides, he's missing the most important parts of the story.

All he knows is that he got out of that state quickly – the minute he took a leak, threw up, splashed his face with water, made up a lie about having left his wallet in his other trousers, and escorted her out into the street. She pressed herself against him as if afraid of the dark, in some ridiculous romantic performance, putting her head on his shoulder and shoving her hands into his pockets without asking, and he kept quickening his pace, pushing his hands into his armpits and cursing the late hour and the cold, complaining that spring should have arrived a long time ago. Suddenly he was sober and way behind, and he no longer had any will to finish this chapter. Everything was back to its old place, his head nailed upside down, his car slapped with a parking ticket. But it was only fair to put his arms around her, at least that, and drive her home, and then also pull over halfway there and do what he had to do, fumble around with her breasts, mess up her clothes, ram his face into her hair and pull her beneath him with his last atom of strength, and unzip his trousers, panting, to show her that he really wanted to, he really did, but try as he might he couldn't dig the worm out of his boxers, and it was a matter of common decency to ask for a rain check, with as much conviction as he could muster, dictate her the wrong phone number and write down hers with feigned attention, and then wait patiently until she was inside the building, giving her a chance to turn and wave at him, as if he would really come back, tomorrow or soon, as if he couldn't wait, and then he would settle that bill along with the rest of his karmic debts and would not end up being a bastard who puts it all off until some better time, in one of their next lives after the many deaths to come.

8

WHEN THE SUN FINALLY CAME OUT, people walked out onto their balconies and almost broke into applause. And even though the stains and dust were more visible in the bright light, their heating bills went down, they could save on gas and public transport, go on a coatless stroll around the city, and have a beer on a park bench. The mud receded into the floorboards, radiant light draped their eyelashes, blazing even in the dark, there was no need to turn the lights on, they didn't close the windows either, there was nothing to hide or dim, they just lay next to each other without a single shot fired, and it suddenly seemed there was nothing easier than love, and that life was, after all, just a bunch of easily attainable little things which should, therefore, be observed from a meteorological perspective. After the rain comes sun, or something like that.

In the garden over at the convent, eiderdowns were being aired, the slope was teeming with primroses and bluebells, and the nuns, like a flock of magpies, pecked around the yard, tying up fruit trees and singing about God's mysterious ways. The neighbour had refreshed the flower beds in front of the building entrance. He'd brought in a dozen sacks of earth, and using some planks he built a cascading planter, then put in different coloured flowers on each level. He pulled out the rotten cypresses and dug several new holes on each side of the driveway to fill the tree line, where the new silver cedars were to be planted. He provided each tenant with a detailed landscaping plan, as well as a bill for their share in the cost of the seedlings. They paid it right away. Suddenly this was possible, too. The money fell from the sky. He was offered a writing gig at a free local newsletter distributed in trams and delivered to letterboxes, and she got a job through an agency that organised events at film premieres. Every Thursday, when the lineup at the cinemas changed, she'd put on a costume and make a fool of herself. But other people did far worse, with jobs that made them look like complete idiots, asses, mules, billboards, doormats, umbrella holders, hangers, rags, brushes and other consumables; or with no jobs at all, digging through rubbish bins, cursing themselves under their breath, only to kick the bucket without much fanfare. It wasn't their turn yet but they could well be next, because tomorrow the weather might break, the sky might open and rain down locusts, cats and dogs, and they might wake up again penniless, with no one to take pity on them; hungry and angry like bears, and yet, on the other hand, something beautiful and completely illogical could happen too, because God's ways were mysterious indeed; and so they observed the rolling clouds from their balcony with optimism, and they went on spending money while they had it, and they thanked God for the ridiculous thing that took place every Thursday.

Depending on the occasion, they'd dress her up as an alien, a panda or a bride of Dracula, with her eyelids painted black and a mouthful of plastic fangs; they'd give her basic instructions and a voucher for free popcorn and position her in front of a publicity backdrop with sponsor logos for the celebrity guests' pictures to be taken with her teeth in their necks. She would bulge up her eyes, open her plastic prosthesis wide, and bite.

It was supposed to be funny, especially when they brought in the president. He arrived in the company of a lady and a bodyguard once the police had secured the theatre, ID'd the staff and sealed all the openings in the walls. They sat him down at a prearranged spot; he loosened his tie, pulled down his collar and cracked some stupid joke that made the crowd in the lobby laugh; and she leaned over, close to his ear, his shirt, the orange foundation stain lining his collar; she swallowed hard, opened her mouth wide, and pretended to suck his blood while waiting for the photographer to wrap it up. The crowd was still in stitches as he congratulated her on her role and held out his sweaty palm, pulling it back into his jacket sleeve the very next second and heading for the auditorium before she could respond. He didn't even shake her hand; he merely wiped his on hers. The whole thing lasted no more than a minute, yet he managed to convey the message that he too was only human, with sweaty temples, shirt and palms; that he too was tired of his own crap, that is, his job; that he no longer had the patience to listen to what the people had to say, to what she might say to him, which was basically that things were bad and they weren't going to get any better for them, but neither would they improve for him, because sooner or later he'd have to explain where all those people, money and factories had gone, and what it was he'd done to deserve all the huge banquets, private plane trips and perks, what the fuck he'd done with all his fucking time, since he couldn't think of an honest answer now, and did he really think he was doing something valuable, offering his lifeless palm around, now to her as well, at a hygienic distance – her, an actress who could clearly see the panic behind his gestures and jokes? That was the message.

He who works will make mistakes.

He will make mistakes, yet he will still keep working.

But what goes around comes around.

It comes around, or maybe it doesn't.

And so people laugh, to be on the safe side.

During the reception, she would change in the toilet, take off her makeup and wash her armpits, and exchange the costume for an envelope of cash behind the sponsor's banner. She'd try not to feel like shit. She would shove the envelope deep into her bag, squeeze it close to her body, make her way through the crowd in the lobby, and take the escalator down to the ground floor. The glass door would open automatically for her, and outside it would already be Friday, midnight would have passed, street cleaners would be sweeping the road, and God, still blind to human suffering, would be scattering petals all over the pavement.

Tonight she's playing the queen from some historical movie in which she ultimately gets beheaded. They have powdered her face and bust, dressed her up in a couple of petticoats, stuck her in a wig, painted on a black mole, and planted her at the theatre entrance to hand out sponsors' leaflets and greet people in French; she has to be careful not to lose her wig or rip her dress, and to get the accent right, if possible; and after the screening, in timely fashion, she'll have to strike a pose by the banner with the logo of the company that supplied the premiere with wine, cheese and sausages, under the slogan 'Welcome to a European banquet'. There they will arrange her between two sky-blue flags sprinkled with yellow stars, put a tray of canapés in her hands and then turn on the fans – and when the flags straighten up and start fluttering to form something like the hull of a ship, she will fix her body as the figurehead on its bow, and then, with the sails filled with wind and the passengers' stomachs filled with food, she will steer the vessel westward, towards the future, towards a better tomorrow, which, make no mistake, will indeed start tomorrow, with a free barbecue and cultural programmes at the main city square, culminating in a spectacular ceremony on the occasion of joining the European Union, when the assembled statesmen will reassert the very same idea; that we have boarded this metaphorical ship; that after an arduous and fearful trip, our collective dream has finally come true; and that now it's time to wake up.

Meanwhile she can do whatever she wants, loiter around the lobby, watch the trailers for upcoming blockbusters, the quick shots of sex and exploding cars, close-ups of actresses staring intently and trying hard to cry, wondering if she'd really be where she is now if she could play the scenes any better; but then she'll remember to be kinder to herself and not to ask such questions, because there are people far more mediocre out there than her, people with much less talent, who'd give their right arm to be in her shoes, bored out of her mind, despising herself, and still making money. And historical movies never seem to end. There's still a revolution to be won, aristocracy to be to overthrown, new cadres to be appointed, an old regime to be reinstalled under a different name, closing the circle, and only then will there be time for a piss followed by a wine-and-cheese reception.

She could slip to the toilets and have a fag. The smoke alarms aren't working in there. She studies the graffiti in the last stall to the right, chain-smoking. She's thinking of a ship laden with abundance. And of an iceberg piercing its hull, a lever hitting the fuel tank and causing a fire, a giant wave carrying the passengers off the overloaded deck, and the morning after. The lucky survivors will soon find themselves in the same line at the job centre. Everyone meets there eventually. They'll have a coffee from the vending machine, exchange complaints and curses, agree that they've been tricked, fucked over, robbed and forgotten, and then they'll feel a little bit relieved, because they're not perishing alone – the whole country is sinking with them. And this now sounds ridiculous, especially from the perspective of a queen who was beheaded for similar crimes.

WE DON'T NEED ANYTHING – THEY PROMISED US EVERYTHING!

That's the writing on the toilet wall.

She could chuckle at this 'til the cows come home, but then she hears the stampede of heels piercing their way to the toilets, and the splash of urine on toilet seats. She puts out her cigarette and rushes out of the stall, walking past the string of trinkets, purses and jackets waiting in line to have a piss, and then she pauses, despite her haste; she stops and turns around, as if hearing someone call her name, as if expecting someone to tug at her sleeve, right now, and ask her what she's doing there behind that ludicrous mask, what's with the dress and the mole, and what the hell has been going on with her since she disappeared from the face of the earth and locked herself away in that stage set with couch. She'd really like someone to ask her this, for someone to speak to her, to return her gaze so she can launch into the monologue she's long prepared before the kitchen tiles, and show them how superbly she can deny the most obvious state of things, especially clothes; how she can wear her costume coolly like jeans and lie recklessly, say she has better things to do, say she's spent her time breathing and meditating, practicing yoga, reading Dante and doing work on herself, with monumental results that, true, she hasn't been able to show to anyone, but then wave it all off casually as if that didn't bother her one bit, because doubtlessly her moment would come, too; perhaps with a slight delay, just as spring came eventually, but then she would finally shine. She'd just love to utter those few sentences and then cut the conversation short with a casual smile and a remark that it's a long story, which in fact is true; it's long and tedious, and it's highly unlikely anyone would care to hear it, just as it's unlikely anyone would speak to her, ask her about the dress, the mole and the wig, her health or her life, because a life like hers holds little interest to anyone, a costume like hers can hardly fascinate anyone, it's the kind of role that doesn't get applause, and such conversations would demand grace and time that remain unavailable, especially now, when sandwiches are already being served and everyone has more important matters to attend to, like their lips and eyelashes in the mirrors on the walls, where they can see their powdered heads among many other powdered heads in the same reflection, with hers grotesquely standing out in this cosmetics scene, paler, bigger and incongruously sad; and it's now also weighing so heavy that she can barely hold it on her shoulders, feeling the inner burden pulling it down, and it's only a matter of seconds before it unnaturally tilts to the side and, cut off, falls to the tiles.

Like in the movie.

It landed on its crown and rolled under the sink, bloodless and silent, but instead of picking it up from the floor right away, she simply turned her back on it and proceeded to leave, as if not surprised at all, as if it were perfectly normal for a body to walk without its own head when it's doing what the head would rather not do, not even for an envelope of cash, so she diligently trotted to the flags in the lobby, obediently took the previously arranged pose, and sailed off to hell. She fluttered with the wind in her sails for an hour and more, never moving from the spot, with the moronic tray in her hands, until the fans switched off and the glasses emptied and they informed her it was Friday and she could go home, told her there would be no premieres next week, and maybe not even a week after that, but not to worry because they'd keep her in mind and call her as soon as there was something on the horizon. Only then did she go to fetch her head, which was still lying on the toilet floor, trampled and marked by footprints, with dirty paper towels sticking to her face as it stared at the door, looking towards the crowd of refined people totally absorbed in some other rubbish, unlikely to pay attention to her smallness under their shoes, unlikely noticing the abandoned head observing them from below, unlikely to wonder, for instance: is it their imagination, or is she really crying? She'd had a hard fucking day.

She didn't have to say anything else. She found him in the kitchen, comparing data on water usage in city fountains, and drafting an article for the newspaper. She drew her hand across her throat, and he got the message, loud and clear. As of tomorrow, the weather is changing. A new civil war is starting. He'll be needing a helmet and a bulletproof vest, because now he'll be blamed for everything again. But there's no helping it; he knows that by now, as he tries to pull her into his arms, squeezing her like a broom or a chair or a dried-up tree, whispering in her ear that they're not poor after all, because they've got arms and legs and hearts and genitals, they have that couch, too, which is enough to do something for themselves, to have a good fuck and see if things will feel different afterwards, because if you ask him, the problem is not the money – there's plenty of money to be thrown around and poured into fountains, according to his data, and thus, according to the law of probability, it's bound to trickle down to them, too. But it's all in vain, him assuring her that these are proven facts, that money flows, that fucking heals, because she doesn't care for it, she doesn't care for anything, she's had a difficult Thursday – how many times does she have to tell him? She leans out the window, now hanging over the neighbour's garden with him awkwardly holding her from behind, her breasts in his fists; and he's not an idiot, of course he heard her say she didn't care for it, she didn't have to tell him twice, but he can't let go, he can't move away, because he feels like something might fall again.

9

SHE HUNG LIKE THAT FROM THE WINDOW for several nights, trying to focus on the maths and make a calculation in which zero times zero would result in a positive sum; trying to figure out what to do tomorrow, the day after tomorrow, and the rest of her life, which, lo and behold, went on even when there was nowhere to go, crushing objects, people and surfaces as if they were cast from plaster, there being a very small probability life would not squash them this time. Such are statistics. The percentage of citizens subsisting on air had exceeded fifty percent of the total number, and along came an announcement of benefit cuts, more budget cuts and expert job cuts, as well as the introduction of tax on walking, breathing and digestion. For real. And it didn't matter that they'd tightened their belts down to the size of a noose, for other people had done the same, and yet they fell victims to a depressed market, physically alive yet economically dead, dragging through the streets wrapped in red maternity coats they'd found in the rubbish. And she didn't have to feel guilty for having no change or sympathy to spare, turning her head away from them as if from a TV report on some natural disaster, because that was exactly how it was, like a sequence of strong seismic shocks considered an act of nature, so no compensation could be claimed.

A man without a home is an everyday occurrence.

Just like a man without a job. Or a man without a head.

What good would it do him?

And anyway, zero resists multiplication, as well as imagination and any kind of meditation. And so he doesn't even bother; he stares at the crack in the wall, at the ruins behind that wall that sprang from a similar crack, at the rot spreading over those remains, at the long recovery process that he fails to envisage, and he smokes. He's sitting propped on his elbows over an ashtray full of cigarette butts, blowing out smoke rings and calmly observing the crack swelling in the floorboards; and he still wouldn't move if the ceiling were to collapse on his head. So once again, she'll have to tell him it can't go on this way, it's high time he did something concrete; got off his arse, sold a kidney, went down to the betting shop, or at least called the fire department, and he will nod his head as if agreeing, actually get up, step over the crack between the kitchen and the living room, and go to bed like a rational man who can't do a thing to stop an earthquake.

And as reasonable as this may have been, he'll have to answer for that act for days to come, because the very next morning she'll accuse him of abandoning her at the moment when her foundations, that is, her nerves, gave way, when she had a very concrete feeling that she was losing ground, and that she was going to fall through the cracks along with the furniture, and the neighbours would once again start leaving notes in their letterbox about the intolerable ruckus they're making, and threaten to call the police. She'll follow him closely like despair, as he puts on his socks, as he washes his face, as he takes a piss, she'll scratch at the bathroom door, and through the keyhole she'll complain to him about having spent all night mending the cracks in the floor and putting the kitchen together, with her back holding up the walls; she'll use hyperbole and metaphor, counting on his correct interpretation, on him understanding what it was that pushed her to the edge, to want to hang herself by the zero-size noose, to jump out the window and thus do something reasonable herself, even if it incurred additional medical costs, but she didn't do it, and he should be thanking her for that instead of shutting the door in her face, she didn't do it because of him, because of the child, because of the love that's made of pure gold so she can pawn it until they get out of this shit, until she finds a job that suits her qualifications, and she can finally cash in on years of gruelling work during which she donned other people's lives for free, rehearsing roles that were greater, louder and far more universal than this one of hers; learning them by heart in case she ever needed them, in case she got a chance to show how much taller and louder she can be, how she can multiply, become a symphony orchestra, a pneumatic drill, a fire in a theatre, which of course no one ever asked her to do, they just hammered her into the stage like a nail into a board, killed her zeal by giving her tasks a circus monkey could perform; slip, fall, show her knickers and keep her legs up in the air as long as possible; and they never even tried to hide the fact that it was a circus, that they had no interest in art, but rather only in very exact material relations; how many bums on seats per play, that is, how much turnover per actor. Or per monkey. They assured her the audience wouldn't tolerate art either; all the questioning, uncertainties, hidden meanings and open endings, they weren't interested in what could be done with hearts and words, only what arses and bare hands could do, it was the latter that touched their soul, which is why she acted only with her arse and her fists, going on stage as if before a firing squad, anxiously waiting for the play to end, surrounded by colleagues who suffered from the same affliction, obliged to play monkeys, clowns or drunks, often also becoming them, screaming and sputtering at the front rows, trampling over their own feet, flapping their hands and slapping themselves on the face, just like they were told to, comforting themselves with the thought that the rubbish they're giving to the people is the rubbish the people are asking for, because people like to hear a juicy curse and the whack of a slap, they love to see a hard fall and a broken neck, they don't pay admission to have their soul fed or their heart torn to pieces, they pay to snigger at others' misery, gloat over others' bruises, look at the morons ten times more pathetic than themselves, and finally leave the theatre convinced they have it good in their own skin.

So this was her job, to deceive people, even before he knocked her up and moved his couch in, even before she thought love could make up for everything and so she could quit and wait for a better chance, a miracle for which she would charge three times the price, the magical five minutes that would fulfil her and inspire her, and she would fly out of her costume like a dove from a magician's hat, turn a somersault in mid-air and show them all.

Oh well.

It's best she turns her back on both the kitchen and the couch and pulls herself together by looking at solid constructions: the thick walls of the convent, the firmly planted crucifix by the path to the chapel, the deeply rooted silver cedars that the neighbour is now watering and will probably serve them with a bill for later. But she should forgive him like a good Christian, because the neighbour's insomnia may well be more severe than hers, he can't take his head off and put it back in place as needed, he suffers it twenty-four hours a day, so when his head tells him to go out in the middle of the night, he actually pulls his trousers on over his pyjamas, and goes out to make sure each and every bud is still in its place on the branch, and to check if the vandals digging through the communal waste bins in the dark have broken any of his saplings or trampled over his flower beds, out of sheer malice, annoyed with him for planting flowers instead of potatoes, because they hate everything that's inedible, and also beautiful, everything that grows, thrives and buds, whereas they can barely afford a bread roll. And he is well aware of the fact that people have little love for aesthetics, as they have little love for their neighbour, his property or his garden, and so as soon as he hears the piercing screech of the metal waste bin being gutted again, he quickly gets out of bed and rushes out on patrol, as he used to do during the war, except armed with a pistol back then instead of a watering hose, checking the blackout was being observed and firing at the windows whose blinds leaked light. And never for a moment did he doubt his sacred mission, the idea that he was part of a grand and sometimes incomprehensible plan in which there were no mistakes or coincidences, and according to which man gets only what he deserves, a bullet in the window if needed, for that was the will of God, and he believed back then as he believed now that he was on the side of the weak and powerless, those who couldn't protect themselves, for a man will fall and rise again, a man will be spat upon and clean himself, a man will bleed and the wound will heal, whilst the flowers will perish because of their innocence, because they grow quietly and are broken easily. If you asked him, people should be growing tulips and roses instead of having children. That would make for less despair and misery in the world, and less of the poor to undermine the economy and steal food from honest workers' mouths, and fewer vandals like these who hook shit out of the waste bins and drag it around the parking lot.

Trash, says the neighbour.

And he's not talking about the plastic, milk cartons or gooey remnants of God knows what; he's talking about human scum that should be washed off the streets with a hose. Each and every last one of them. But the neighbour is mistaken in assuming that man is equivalent to the shit he digs through, and that he can just be flushed away with a hose; the neighbour is mistaken in thinking if he does this, if he really sprays the man, the man wouldn't stick the hose up his arse, as he's told him he would, two or three times already, he warned him to turn off the bloody water and mind his own business, but the neighbour didn't listen to the voice of reason, he trusted his own assessment that counted on the help of a higher power entangled with the contents of the grand plan, and he also saw the crucified Jesus on the convent slope and he saw eyes in the windows of the building, and idiotically concluded that God would certainly not forsake him in front of so many witnesses. But he should have remembered that God's hands were nailed down and that He couldn't help him even if He wanted to, whereas the rest of them really didn't want to, it was the last thing on their minds as they didn't give a toss about the neighbour's herbs, or his arse, much as he didn't give a toss about the bullet holes in their windows; the only thing that troubled them was the hectolitres of water steadily gushing out onto the asphalt, but since it was a matter of collective responsibility, everyone assumed someone else would turn it off.

The neighbour took it with dignity; the moment they grabbed him he went speechless and surrendered without a struggle. Maybe he wanted to appear as gracious as he believed himself to be, in front of the other building residents, or he really expected that heavenly lightning would strike at the last moment and burn the hands that seized him by his belt and collar, carried him across the parking lot and dumped him in a communal waste bin like another putrid rubbish bag. They dropped him head-first into the sludge at the bottom, and his whole body squashed the bin contents, which exploded in all directions. He rolled over and got on his knees so as not to suffocate, clutching at the edge of the waste bin in panic. He kept his eyes and mouth tightly shut, as a trickle of unspeakable muck ran down his face, and when they hit him in the chest with an iron hook and slammed the metal lid on his fingers, what hurt him the most was the fact that, as he opened his mouth to scream, he swallowed the muck. They wheeled the bin towards the slope lined by rows of residential buildings, descending to the intersection to the city centre, and – cursing his mother and sister – they pushed him down the hill. They knew not what they did, it seemed. And although it didn't absolve them from guilt, the biblical quote suited the occasion, for the neighbour was kneeling with his arms outstretched with crushed fingers, with a symbolic bruise on his heart, humiliated and deserted, and when the bags full of shit shook and spun around like in a lottery machine, and when the wheels of the bin reached their full speed and the noise grew thicker than the stench, he knew what was coming, he couldn't believe it but he knew: he would jump a red light, trigger a car to brake, metal would hit metal, and the flowers and silver cedars would wither sometime later. A man will be killed, and a man will rise again, he kept saying to himself, and it hurt less.

And as the neighbour rolled down towards his declining destiny, and the angels started singing over the intersection, she quietly stepped into the room where the child and the rag doll bunny were sleeping, to look for the man lying in half light. He was still awake, his arms crossed behind his head, staring at the smooth paint of the ceiling. There isn't a single crack in it any more, he whispered as she entered. Not one, she confirmed, and lay down as close to him as she could, thinking about how all it took for the walls to heal and for the hollow loop of zero to fill with some hope was a little cruelty, just a tiny portion of it, a cursory glance at someone who's having it incomparably worse, for her to suddenly feel so good in her own skin.

10

YOU CLOSE YOUR EYES AND YOU FALL, deeper and deeper, dropping a few metres lower with each breath, at the speed of a body in free fall; you hear the buzz of pressure in your ears, the feeble resistance of the abyss, and then you crash-land on the couch. This is as low as it goes. The height from which you fell is about as high as the top floor of the tallest skyscraper in the city, the corporate headquarters for which your wife used to shoot commercials; from up there there's a beautiful view of the suburbs, the motorway arteries penetrating the neighbourhoods and forking through concrete sleeping spaces, and the road heading in from the south with its spectacular array of fountains programmed to change colours and water effects. The view doesn't say much, except that people, observed from an elevated perspective, truly look like ants carrying heavy loads for the equivalent of a bread crumb; all they're left with when the fountains are deducted from their income. You explained all this much better in your article, in your detailed analysis of the murky flow of investments through the newly installed water pipeline, comparing its actual length with the fivefold cost of the invoiced materials, and you dug up the nepotist roots between the clients and the contractors, and sketched out the dense map of black holes in financial statements that sucked in twenty million in public money, with the ants' meek consent. You thought you were finally doing something honest and constructive, in the name of justice, in the name of a salary that will pay the rent and prevent the next kitchen earthquake; you kept calling the editor, pestering his secretary; you expected compensation for overtime and overwork, for a ton of miscellaneous material which you brought to the surface, separating the soil from the shit and arranging it into a readable structure, in chronological order and with names named; you kept on calling, convinced it was much easier to publish than to dig up all that dirt from the pipeline, and in the end you found yourself knocking on the editor's office door, proudly clenching a shovel in your hands. You arrived there soaring, burning with reformist zeal, like a bird with a two-metre wingspan and ten grams of brain clad in down, which – surprisingly – failed to signal to you that you'd land on a branch you'd already sawn off, or rather, that you'd fall into a grave you'd dug yourself. At the office they handed you a copy of the city newsletter hot off the press – you flipped through it impatiently, from the front and from the back, thoroughly checking each headline, title and notice, and you learned about the upcoming long-awaited grand opening of the underground car park accompanied by a tamburitza music programme; you learned that the city has invited tenders for a conceptual design project to convert public toilets on the main square into an aquarium; and you learned that your article wasn't printed nor will it ever be; that the editor is too busy to see you and doesn't want to be disturbed today or tomorrow or ever, because he'll be too busy, of course he will… you idiot. And that was the moment you closed your eyes and let yourself fall down onto the good old couch, but before you rammed your face into the fabric and cried like your own child, and before you took a nosedive onto the pavement in front of the underground car park.

Haven't you had enough?

There are about thirty of you lying on the ground next to each other, your faces turned to the sky as if on a beach; the sky is clear and an old street lamp is swaying, hung on the line, arching above the passage between the buildings. You'd never noticed it before. You couldn't have, she'd tell you, you shouldn't have, because you don't have the luxury of lounging on barricades, protesting against the devastation of cultural heritage and public space as if it were your battle that you can actually afford. Don't act dumb, she'd add – you know very well there's a fundamental and crude priority difference between the struggle for bread and the struggle for transparent urban planning, and that the latter can compromise the former, which you could and should have learned fiom the example of your one and only unpublished article demanding wages and justice; you wanted to have your cake and eat it too, instead of deciding what you need more, which battle is easier to lose, keeping in mind the fact that one fight has already been lost and the case has been closed; construction documents have been approved, signed and locked away in drawers that no one will be looking through anymore, and in no more than a quarter of an hour the tamburitza band standing by the ticket machine will start banging on the strings. All they're waiting for is the TV crew.

She'd sharpen the hook of the question mark and drive it straight into your back.

What the fuck are you fighting for, then?

You're all holding hands and blocking the line of cars waiting to turn into the car park. Traffic has stopped moving. The cars waiting to drive straight on are honking at the cars that now can't turn right. Several journalists on site are reporting that the gridlock outside the entrance has blocked the traffic in the entire city centre, with special police units expected to arrive soon. Someone whispers in your ear not to get up; when the police

85

arrive, you'll offer passive resistance. They'll take you all to the police station to get your personal details, and then they'll let you go. You'll all be on the evening news. You nod. But of course you're nodding, you aaaaant, she'd sneer at you now, stretching that first vowel into a limp earthworm, all stupefied when it gets trampled on the pavement; of course you're nodding because you don't have the guts to go home with the sawn-off branch under your arm; you're ashamed to admit you're wasting time when you should just get up and head for the tram, in the face of your supine comrades possibly booing you and calling you a coward, accusing you of spreading civic apathy, and they would certainly do this, because unlike you, they don't ponder over bread crumbs, they ponder over concepts, ideas and strategies, and they can lie there until the next morning because they don't have a hook in their back.

Not all ants are the same – a complicated and painful thought that makes you feel like a traitor and that prevents you from surrendering to the wave of collective euphoria that heats up the atmosphere to carnival heights the moment the police and TV crew all arrive at the same time to the soundtrack of tamburitza, making you all blush from stage fright. And now you're breaking into song. The intervention team will take you all into the van, handling you with care as if you were babies or boxes of crystal glasses. Each person boarding the van will make room on the bench for the next, because you've all agreed beforehand what this TV report will look like, with all protagonists respecting the procedural consensus upon which democracy rests, and you're collaborating on a joint project, which in turn relieves any surface tension and transforms capitulation into celebration. Three minutes on the evening news will illustrate the graceful conduct of civil society and the plural, tolerant and civilised system in which people sing even as they are taken into custody. But you, little ant, you aren't singing and you're not in a celebratory mood, and you don't give a fuck about them using the least possible force on you, or that they may even offer you coffee at the station; you don't give a fuck about your comrades revelling in media attention which will raise public awareness by zero point one percent, about them taking pictures against the partition cage inside the van and tagging each other on social media, and cracking up when three cops drop a fat guy halfway to a parked vehicle because they have to rest; you don't give a fuck that everyone except you is overjoyed, because you just lay there yet again and did nothing. And this is the kind of luxury, remember, that you can't afford.

That's what she'd say to you.

Wake up.

And now's the moment to break free from your state of hypnosis and smash the fucking matrix, the way only you can, against your own and the common good, violating all agreements; despite the feeling of powerlessness you've been carrying from the anthill, and despite the obvious disproportion in strength, you'll offer unexpected resistance by performing an epileptic seizure in the hands of the police, in front of the horrified comrades who can't believe what an imbecile they had among their ranks, and the seeming cohesion will disintegrate. The man will explode when he least expects to explode, he'll fight back after the fight is over, with a serious delay, distrusting the comradeship, the meaning, the song, turning into a common ogre who doesn't understand the protocolar nature of the struggle, its discursive militancy and practical pacifism; he resists, he roars, he thrashes about, and he trades his lofty aspirations for base instincts, for example at the moment when – amid the chaos of squeezing and gripping – he feels his left trainer slip off his foot, and instead of admitting defeat, he starts struggling and biting even harder, finally finding clear motivation. At the same time, he's hollering as if he's being slaughtered, howling for them to give him back his trainer, yelling about having funded the police with his own money, just as he funded his shoes with his own money, and there were no funds left for a new pair; he's screaming that he wants to talk to the mayor, the prime minister, the president and his editor, asking where's all the scum, all those thieves and mercenaries, and so on, totally incoherent, and making no sense. Finally, they shove him in the van with the others and handcuff him.

The Lord giveth and the Lord taketh away – the saying is correct, but because your loss is so insignificant within the sum of collective losses and the shit you're all in together, your comrades are staring at your sock without pity. If they were you, they'd die of shame. But you can't, you have a family; three mouths, six hands and six feet, one of which is unshod, but you'll cry about that one later. When you throw yourself on your usual spot at the bottom of the world, and your bare-bottomed child climbs on your chest, pushing little arms and legs at the crumbled rock of a father, then letting out a stream of urine and pissing all over you, without malice, simply because the child couldn't hold it. Just like you couldn't hold it either when you had to piss and shit on everything around you.

You couldn't help yourself.

You told them so at the police station, too. They took your fingerprints and personal information, and you waited for them to write you up for public nuisance; you signed a piece of paper and were given a plastic bag that you put on your foot, and then they let you go, straight to the bottom again, and sliding homeward you measured the depth of your downward trajectory, in steps, and in the cost of the upcoming court proceedings, and you regretted they hadn't beaten the shit out of you, and that you hadn't passed out, because then they might've not let you walk home, that's how you're thinking and calculating; and on top of it all you end up bursting into tears over such bullshit, in front of the child who doesn't understand that it bears no blame for your tears, for the short circuit between your expectations and actual impossibilities, for the blood vessel that burst in your brain when you realised you meddled in things you shouldn't have, for the uncontrollable outburst of rage that followed but which missed its target, for that colossal waste of energy akin to the squirting of the water in the fountains that started the whole thing, for the eruption of madness, bitterness and misery that would soon be witnessed by a few million viewers, in less than half an hour, on the evening news; but again, the child doesn't understand this complicated chain of events that can lead to a nervous breakdown, the child just thinks you don't love him, that he gets on your nerves and bothers you, for you haven't kissed, hugged or tickled him; you just handed him all drenched in piss to his mother, and you locked yourself in the bathroom, sobbing, under the pretext that you needed to wash up, which you didn't do at all, you just sat there on the toilet weeping like a woman, wiping your nose with toilet paper, with the tap on so no one could hear you; and, again, the child couldn't have known it wasn't because of him, but simply because you didn't want him to see you like that, even though he would, on the evening news, see a dad cursing his motherland, car park and fountains, as protest organisers try to explain that it's a peaceful protest against the way public space is governed; a dad who is, however, loudly disputing everything they're saying, and expending enormous effort to achieve nothing; a dad dragging his foot wrapped in a plastic bag and not looking at people passing by; a dad so riddled with shame that he can't get out of the bathroom, and who wouldn't survive another person addressing him today, and so he urgently needs to hide inside a third person, the person who just lies on the couch, gathering dust and saying nothing, thinking nothing, trying nothing, and even touching nothing, because, as she's already stated a few times, he would only break something.

11

SHE IS A BULLDOZER pushing junk into a pile, a broom sweeping the dust, hydrochloric acid that will dissolve lime-scale, and a hard brush that will scrub the apartment to the bone before they leave. She is also the nausea with which she'll sort through the items in the pile, separating the useful from the useless, tearing them from the whole and then rearranging them into neat shapes that fit into bags and boxes. Only, she still doesn't know what to do with the couch and the man pulling it around on a leash. Nor with the child confusedly sniffing around the lost territory, following a familiar scent that would lead him, for example, to his cot, which now lies disassembled and bundled with rope next to a packed duffel bag that she labelled with the word 'bedding'. Inside, suffocated under a pillow, the rag doll bunny is having its final rest. The child is trying to sniff it out, opening the bag, digging through its soft grave and pulling it to the surface, and although he doesn't understand death, the child still feels that something is ending, that something is irretrievably lost, and nobody bothers to clarify or tell him about what is gained, because his parents are preoccupied with more important things and are afraid of starting crucial conversations, which would destroy them now; but the child doesn't know how fragile they are, so he crawls back to them, holding his dead friend by the ear, as if he still wants them to explain what happened to the cot, to all the toys and the people, where they are going and why, what decisions were made at the secret kitchen meeting last night, when a letter of warning from the rankled landlord was read aloud, and when all the sums of all the unpaid bills were added up and an unbearable pile of envelopes was opened, including the third notice on missed payments before their electricity is disconnected, which they had to pay the day before yesterday; the day before yesterday, mother found this funny, so hilarious that she burst into crazy laughter, laughter which truly slid towards insanity, speeding down her spine like a fast train, shaking, roaring and squealing, causing a strange fit of shivers in all her joints, which made father squeeze her close to him, fearing she would dislocate a body part.

And that morning, when the technician came and disconnected their meter, she was still giggling, as she's still giggling now, the train looping on the precipice of madness, somewhat calmer but still dangerously tilted to the side, because she just can't believe the lights aren't on, that the TV won't turn on either, that the fridge is no longer working, that they should urgently throw some dirty towels on the floor so the melting ice doesn't flood the kitchen, and that they're leaving, leaving, leaving, preferably before dark, from no place to nowhere, which was decided just last night, and so she's wrapping bowls and cups in newspaper, placing them in a cardboard box, and – almost beggaring belief – she still hasn't gone off the rails.

How can she explain all this to a child?

Because the child may think this is just a game; of how to bury a bunny, how to stack pots, put smaller ones into larger ones, place the lighter ones on the heavier, how to compress all their belongings down to the size of a car boot and squeeze boards in between the seats. The child probably won't miss the walls or the furniture, not in the way that he, for example, will be missing his couch; a tame fabric beast in whose embrace he was able to crush the world into absolute nothingness, to cancel it out during the greatest earthquakes, floods and storms, by shutting his eyes to the scrambled picture, which he would love to do right now, too, to land on its soft back, turn the leash into reins and ride off into the dusk, if he could, thus also undoing the scene that follows, when the sun sinks over the horizon and the rider is left alone in endless space with no walls, no ceiling, no doors, no windows, no electricity, with a wife and a child unlawfully buckled up together in the front seat, which, like his, can't be reclined because of all the boxes stacked in the back. But the child is certainly not thinking about the future, nor about the past; he lacks the historical experience of those thousand plus years, the view of the purple coast, the starry sky that flowed into the sea, and the sparkling sea that rose up to the sky; all those superficial wonders of love that prevented insight into the depths, and his father lying on a rock, the sun burning his back, but nothing hurt and nothing worried him, for he felt he had the whole world in his hands, while mother's hand was on his, on his hair, on his chest, on his worm, on the steering wheel of his bicycle, guiding him first to the left then to the right, and inadvertently playing a disastrous role in their ride through the millennium, of which everyone had their own version, so the child couldn't rely on the facts, but would have to reconstruct the whole story anew based on its outcome, using the mechanisms he has learned so far, driving him to blame others, and to finally speak, at a time when every retreat has been cut off and every withdrawal prevented, to name his own loss, uttering bun-ny, calling bun-ny, blaming them in advance for slamming the door so carelessly, and leaving the keys on the table, forgetting the rag doll bunny that will remain lying somewhere on the floor.

The child goes on to instinctively reproduce the primordial matrix, capable of screaming for days, and he'll do the exact opposite of what he's told, all throughout his childhood and even his whole life, and in line with this learned model he'll keep bringing harm to himself; he'll repeat no, no, no, no, until they slap him, and then he'll curl up into the tiniest ball and break their hearts with his tears, but that won't bring the bunny back, and it won't unlock the door, nor will they unlock it, with those fractures in their chests. The child will dwell in the consequences, in their mud, and won't realise that they're not the same people, that those are not the same walls either; he doesn't know that those walls were once held up by books that sprouted from the floor in thick pillars, rising up all the way to the ceiling, effortlessly opening doors, windows and universes in which everything was possible, without exaggeration, where there was a verified answer for every question and for every quest there was an open road, a companion and a place under the sun, and for every hour of love there was a killer verse, as well as countless new lives for countless such deaths. And then they sold the books for peanuts, down to the last one, Dante, just to fill their stomachs and soon have them empty again, hungry, frightened and startled when the peeling walls of fiction cracked, and the shitty, fucked-up world burst in.

With no poetry.

With no humour.

And no income.

And it wasn't survivable anymore, she told him way back then, we can't live like this, we can't go on like this, and she leaned over wanting him to hug her, nothing more, she swears, but he didn't understand the gesture, he only heard the words, sensed a provocation in them, took a few steps back, his neck hair standing on end as if he had to defend himself, and from this retreat he launched an attack.

Everyone's drowning in shit, he told her, but it's not like he invented it, and he can't just gild it. The economy slides along the amplitudes of growth and crashes; it grows slowly and collapses quickly, and there are no shortcuts in between, he explained to her, as if talking to an idiot; don't look down, you'll get dizzy. And he didn't hug her, he just let her stand there, tilting; he turned on the TV, and for the next few hours he forced her to listen to unintelligent strategies for surviving, living and enduring, as people, factories and cities fall headlong down the sharp curve of statistics. And he felt a little sorry for her, but he also felt edgy, so he held the line, demonstrating military strength that eradicated panic; the art of body and spirit that prepared for clinical death and complete numbness of emotions and thoughts, a skill she would have to practice until she calmed down completely, until, symbolically speaking, she died – as if the world would truly come to its senses when she did, as if he could blame her if she didn't, and even though he didn't want to, he really did blame her, a little later, at the worst moment, when her body started hurting, unbearably, and she curled up around her belly, which no longer provided the mysterious stupor of happiness but a terror beyond imagination, so she gritted her teeth and did what every woman has to do on her own; she breathed in, and pushed out, and when it was finally over and she could see her feet again, she noticed a hole dug up under her feet and, ignoring his instructions, she looked down, down the slope, into the abyss, into the future, and there she saw his body entangled in the curve of economy, and her child hanging next to his corpse, and their lifelong cohabitation in that knot, and their war, and she really felt dizzy and held onto him so as not to fall; and so they slipped together, holding onto each other out of sheer fear, as if to soften the fall, and there they discussed who pushed whom, who gave in first, and they couldn't agree, just like they could no longer

95

love each other, daily, continuously, and she remembered the exact moment she felt he couldn't do it even when drunk, in that hospital room after she gave birth, as she mashed her face in her hands and cried inconsolably, supposedly because of the roses, and he turned on his heel and marched out of the ward as if the only point of her tears was to declare him incompetent and stupid.

And now the train trembles and roars and squeals, and she can smell molten steel dripping from the overheated rails; she can picture the disaster that will follow the moment it exceeds the speed of thought, but she really doesn't know what'll happen an hour or a day later, after they survive; she doesn't even know what should happen now, when everything is packed up and the only thing we can do is have a wash – but we can't predict that either, an invisible brake stops us from thinking beyond the next hour, crossing that threshold, taking that step and leaving the familiar layout of walls and things, because – like a spring – it takes us back to safe ground, where the future is on fucking TV and can be switched off, where debt is abstract, someone else's, or too slow to catch up with us, where the ultimate consequences of insolvency are always deferred and will be passed on to our children and grandchildren, but we won't talk about it because we believe in forgiveness, bully for us, we believe God will throw us a bone at the last moment, and that's why we're not ready to abandon hope, ceiling and floorboards, even in our imagination; we take a bath lit by a candle stuck on a plate in the sink, dress sensibly in layers of clothing, blow out the candle, close the front door, forever, and in the absence of any plan and destination we go to fucking hell, that's right, just like that, like we have no family or friends, like there are no departments, institutes and organisations to protect our right to a dignified life, like we feel guilty suspecting we'd brought it upon ourselves somehow, because we didn't try hard enough, because we were lazy and stupid, because we were in a coma and rose up only when all the alms were already spent, and it was our fault again that it took us too long to react, and so we wouldn't ask for help but would meekly turn the other cheek after all the slaps we'd already received. And here we are in the stairwell, here we are on the road, here we are in the dark, this is our story, we're driving and getting nowhere, it's past dinner time, and it's as if nothing ever happened.

12

SOMEDAY WE'LL LAUGH AT ALL THIS, he said to her
when they got out of the city, after they crossed the plain and
took a local road into the mountains, after they drove for hours
on winding roads through the forest, after she wound down
the window and breathed in the trees, breathed in the ferns,
breathed in the clearings, saying that she needed some air; and
after he said: you know what? and she: what? and he: nothing;
and after she said: maybe we could...? and he: yes? and she:
forget it; and they had nothing more to say, as the white line in
the road dragged them further into the night, without meaning
and without sound, through tunnels and over bridges, and then
abruptly turned downhill, their ears popping with the change in
altitude; and after a rocky landscape stripped bare by the winds
came into view, which meant they were close to the seaside; and
after the red fuel light on the dashboard signalled they were
running on empty, and he yelled: shit! and slammed his fist on
the steering wheel, accidentally hitting the horn; and after she
accused him of waking up the child who wasn't sleeping anyway;
and after she surprisingly apologised to him for being on edge
and they pushed the car to the petrol station, him pushing on
the left and steering through the open window, scuffing those

nice shoes he'd worn at their wedding, and her pushing from behind with her arms outstretched and her body almost parallel to the road; and after they both leaned breathlessly against a service-station barrier behind which a pale morning rose through a mist of salty crystals; and after he went to take a leak, and she turned her back on the dawn to scrape the dirt from her palms, looking towards the motel restaurant where, through the window, she could see tourists carrying trays of toast, eggs and coffee; and after she ran to the motel toilets to freshen up a bit, as she mentioned to him in passing; washing her hands, combing her hair, and polishing her teeth with her index finger; and after she looked decent again, like the other tourists, but not feeling any better; and after she took wet wipes out of her bag and asked him to wipe the child down because she supposedly had to go and do something she forgot the next second, stopping in her tracks between the cars in the middle of the car park, biting her fingernail, staring at people and cars until one of them honked at her, and she jumped away, leaning against the nearest wall, and lighting a cigarette on an empty stomach, as if she really wanted to feel sick; and after the morning turned the sky red and the car bonnets heated up, and for a moment they could believe they would leave their luggage in a hotel room that same afternoon, stick a parasol in the beach and mark the end of the trip, imagining they had stopped here just to empty their bladders and get breakfast; and then, after they actually walked into the restaurant like other families on holiday, loading up trays with food and taking a handwritten receipt as the kind waitress apologised, explaining that the cash register was out of order and they could pay later; after they'd filled up the tank, and the waitress cleaned up a table in the corner for them, brought them a high chair and wished them bon appetit, safe travels and a pleasant summer, and mother took father's hand, caressed the child's cheek and flashed the waitress a dazzling

Hollywood smile that no one could tell she'd acquired through practice; and after the dazzle faded and she forced her breakfast down her constricted throat and made a sandwich from the leftover bread and cheese, wrapped it in a napkin and swept up the crumbs with her palm; and after she sighed, and after he sighed, and they silently played a game of chess with dirty plates and empty cups on a tray, with sweat dripping from his face as if each move was a matter of life or death; and after he finally put an end to the game and leaned over to her, not wanting anyone to hear, he uttered what had been on his mind for a long time: someday we'll laugh at all this.

And, of course, she recognised the sentence – it took her back to the first chapter, to the warm room and the powdery Easter snow flickering through the windows, and it was vital to believe it, to laugh at it, even though her laughter sounded like a screech of a train braking at the sight of damaged rails, whereas his resembled the laughter of a man throwing himself under the same train to stop it with his own body, placing his head in front of her locomotive running at full speed, and her crashing into him, hitting him, and like a ram with its horns trapped, pushing forth even after stopping. That's how it was when they broke down over one seemingly joyful sentence. No one noticed anything. It looked like they were kissing with their foreheads. Or like they'd been shot with a silent bullet, collapsing over dirty dishes with no money to pay for breakfast, with no fuel in the tank, with no room reservation at the resort, no strength to imagine the summer, or autumns and winters marching forth without a break, and all that in front of the child, who couldn't push them apart, or prop them up, or even reach them; he just had to wait, he had to believe his parents were invincible, that nothing could beat or defeat them, that they hadn't died but were merely kissing, and that in a few moments father would push his chair back and stand up, wipe the concussion off his forehead with a single brush of his hand, and head for the restaurant exit, and that mother would fix her hair, carelessly comb her fringe over the consequences of the recent collision, and look around lazily, as if the only things on her mind were the sea, the sun and air mattresses, and smile at the audience sitting at the tables, scattering her glow over all the trays, cups and saucers, and shining brightly across the glass walls, over the blazing car park, over the entire coastline leading all the way to Greece, with jewels rolling over her lips.

And so the child waited. And he believed.

He would go swimming today.

And then father actually stood up and walked through the door, whistling, rolling up his sleeves, and pushed the car to the petrol pump, filled the car up and winked in their direction, as if the real time for laughing was in fact only about to start, just as he was going to signal to mother to grab the sandwich and the child and confidently walk between the tables, scattering her precious stones all around, casting their razor-sharp edges at anyone who'd try to follow or stop them; sidestepping the holes, cliffs and crevices that opened up under her feet as she squeezed the child and counted down the hours it took her to cross the distance between the restaurant and the passenger seat, where he's already waiting, he's started the engine, tapping his fingers on the dashboard, still sweating but stubbornly whistling, a melody bright and unrelated to the suspension of time, and he'll keep whistling until the mother opens the door, stoops and gets in the car, sets the child on her lap, pulls out the seatbelt, and the clock hands now come unstuck; and only now will the kind waitress and two men in petrol station uniforms rush out in front of their car, shouting and waving, forcing their eyes closed against her smile, flashed straight at them, bouncing off the windows and security cameras, as father reverses and turns towards the exit with screeching wheels, determined as if he knows exactly what comes next, as if he's written all of this himself, as if it were really possible to replace reality with words, pull fiction to the surface of the world and decorate it with miracles, reverse the order of things, turn the composition of the landscape upside down, meld sky with islands and sea with clouds, and then paint a woman and a child blue, sprinkle them with gold, pearls and jewels that he now had more than he knew what to do with, and finally do something magnificent; put a full stop right there, turn the wheel, step on it and fly off, all for the sake of love.

Translator's Note

There's a game I sometimes play in Berlin with my friends, ex-pats from the country formerly known as Yugoslavia; we call it the Poverty Pentathlon. We rummage through our childhoods to come up with the most ridiculous – yet always true! – episodes of growing up in destitution. One of us lived without any heating in the house, warming herself at night with a stove-heated roofing tile. 'Yeah, but you had a roof to take the tile off!' someone says, and she loses points. Another one had to move every couple of years, from one terrible landlord or *lady* to the next, intruding into their homes at will, much like swarms of bugs and insects out of the unfinished walls. Here one of us once got bitten by a scorpion, and her mother, a doctor, had to give her a tetanus shot right there, on that bed, a thin two-piece sponge that the whole family of four slept in. The marriage fell apart, there was a lot of shouting and screaming, once there was blood on their mother's nightgown, right down the middle, in line with her nose. There was no other room to put the kids in, so they watched in silence, swallowing the whimpers of their world ending.

The world of Ivana Sajko's *Love Novel* is my world, the world where we are all winners in this wretched competition, clutching our medals as our most precious possessions while they cut into our palms, extending our life lines. Sometimes these lines make for whole books.

Ivana's world being mine made the work of translation both easier and harder. It is not a long book, but it took me over a year to translate it – I broke many deadlines, too many promises, and finally came through only thanks to the support, eternal patience and grace of our editor Katy (you deserve a shout-out, and a crate of best beer!). But you see, every time I opened the book, it was like a punch in the gut. A punch by someone I knew, a family member.

I would translate a sentence (and Ivana's sentences, as you have witnessed, are living organisms – each twisting across the page, demanding you harness it, and have it lead you) – and then I would need a break. Sometimes those breaks between sentences lasted for weeks. Going back to the text was like climbing back into the ring with the most intimidating of fighters. (Think Karate Kid meeting Ivan Drago of *Rocky IV*, if that means anything to you.)

To be sure, a translator needn't have experienced or lived through any of the events; the political, social, class or cultural context presented in the book in order to do a good job – in fact, I'm sure that having all those under your belt can often be an obstacle, feeling the text so close to home, wrecked and ruined, so close that you truly believe that no word in a foreign language can absorb the vast world it is supposed to carry, and birth anew. And this world, you may fear, is just too much, just as it is to live it – it's too much to take for a language that has no word for *tamburitza*, the instrument embodying the tradition and the deepest darkness of our own version of patriarchal conservatism: How do you translate this sound? Into a language that does not know *pelinkovac*, a cheap drink that goes a long way if you want to black out, yet stay on the 'arty' side of the night. (Something like absinth, but not quite). This not-quiteness is something you have to contend with, as a translator, and make peace with, eventually. Befriend, even. Trust that the reader, across the linguistic ocean, doesn't need to have been slapped to feel the sting of the palm across their face, doesn't need to have scars to prove that they too bleed. After all, their own language, ultimately, is also but a poor stand-in for what, outside of all languages, we all get to experience in the lifelong Olympics of Feelings.

***

Funny, when I first read *Love Novel*, just as it was published in Croatian – I read it in a single breath, its avalanche of images and emotions carrying me to the final full stop so smoothly that I barely noticed any words. Funny, I say, because once I started actually looking at the words, as a translator, this whole new world opened up; the incredible network of signals, circular references, compulsive thoughts buried in text to be excavated; the incredible force of the rhythm, carefully curated verbs and nouns, and – my favourite of all Ivana's writerly manoeuvres – her fervent yet seamless switching of tenses, perfectly reflecting patterns of anxious and distressed thought, throwing us back and forth in time, obsessively. It was only when I was given the charge of mediating this book into another language that I was struck by its intricacies, its complexity, and reminded that the art of great writing is to make all the effort invisible. Ivana Sajko has done just that, and I believe – after many rounds in the ring with *Love Novel* – that this translation has done it justice and we have all come out as winners, clutching at our paper medals, right here on this podium of words.

Mima Simić, Berlin, November 2021